I0761318

Living with the Hyenas

Living with the Hyenas

Short Stories by Robert Flynn

Texas Christian University Press
Fort Worth

Acknowledgements

Versions of the following stories have been published previously in periodical form: "Volunteers" in *Blue Mesa Review*; "A Boy and His Dog" in *Concho River Review*; "Living with the Hyenas" in *Concho River Review* and *New Growth 2*; "Flight To Amman" in *New Texas '91*; "Women Don't Know" in *This Place of Memory*; "Reluctant Truth" in *Southwestern American Literature*; and "Defender of the Faith" in *Re: Arts and Letters*.

Library of Congress Cataloging-in-Publication Data

Flynn, Robert, 1932
Living with the hyenas : short stories / by Robert Flynn.
p. cm.
ISBN 0-87565-144-5 (alk. paper)
1. Korean War, 1950-1953 — Fiction. 2. Texas — Social life and customs — Fiction. I. Title.
PS3556.L9L58 1995
813'.54 — dc20
95-8082
CIP

Cover and Text Designed by Barbara Whitehead

Contents

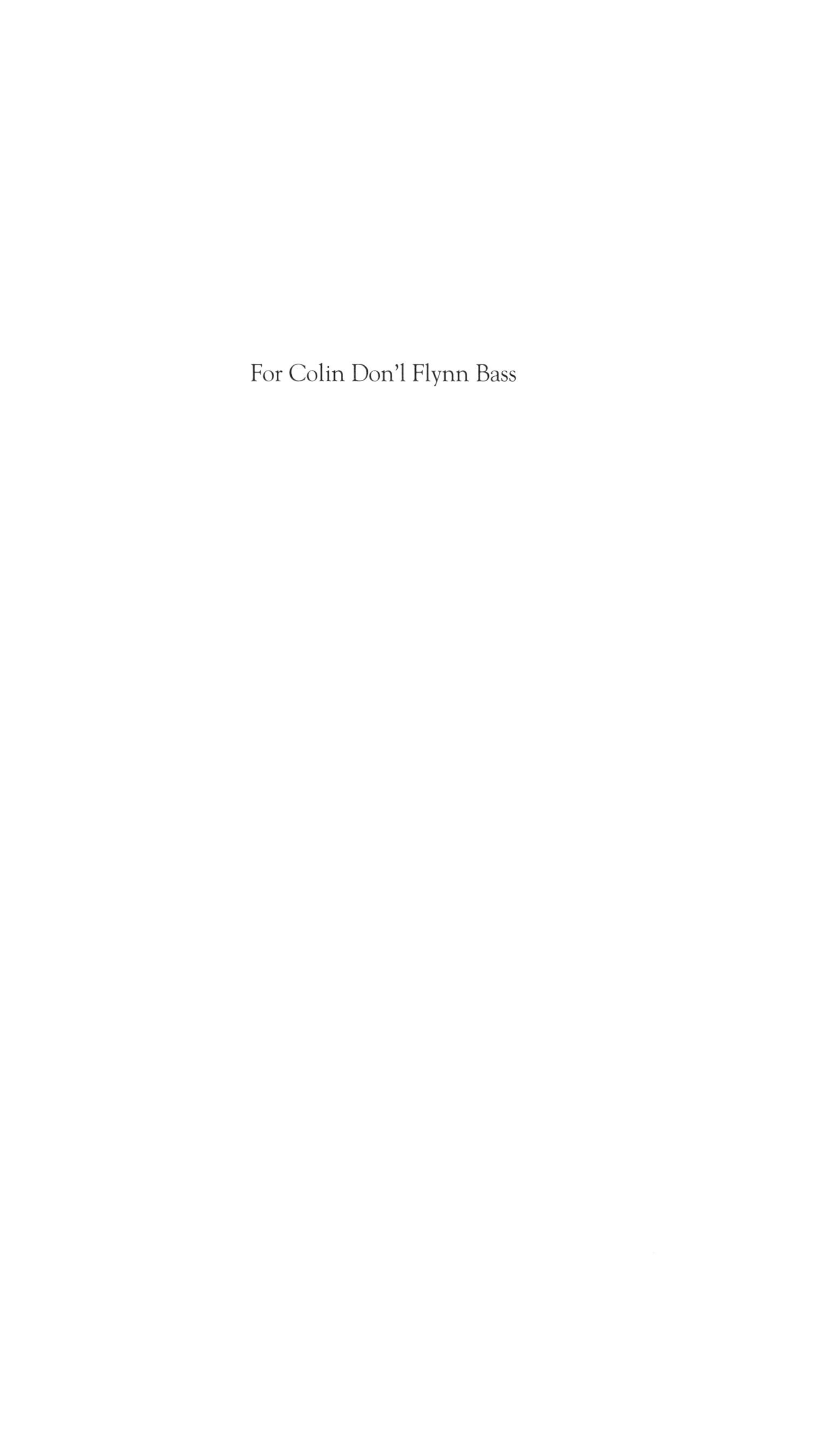

For Colin Don'l Flynn Bass

Foreword

The beginnings of my stories are so small and the process covers such a long period of time that I usually have trouble remembering where a story begins or an idea comes from.

"Land of the Free" was one of those ideas that developed over many years. It began with the memory of a story I heard as a child. An older high school boy was temporarily assigned to drive a school bus. One day he didn't stop to let a girl off the bus, instead pretending he was going to run away with her. The details of the story are hazy, but it was told to me as a joke. Today, it would be sexual harassment, but at the time, it was the kind of rough way that boys teased girls they were attracted to.

The story bothered me, even as a child, maybe because I identified with the victim rather than with the trickster. I first tried to write it from the point of view of a teenage girl whose dignity triumphs over a prankster, but I couldn't get the story going. I moved the story back to the 1930s or '40s, a time when many women could expect male protection, a husband, father or brother to come to their defense. Those stories didn't work either because they escalated toward violence, and I didn't want a resolution by the biggest fist or fastest gun.

I tried writing it from the father's point of view, a father who is unwilling to resort to violence to save his daughter and must find a better way. Those efforts also ended up with the father succeeding through power — political, economic, social or moral power. I gave the motherless girl a father who could not come to her defense, leaving her to her own devices. I experimented with the town drunk, a disabled hero, a charming but inept romantic. Nothing worked.

I made a lot of misbegotten efforts over a lot of years, and I didn't even have the characters or the plot. All I had was an idea about good prevailing over bad, innocence over entrenched power, without resorting to the fastest gun, the biggest bucks or the slickest politician in the West.

I don't know when I decided to make the characters black, or where the idea came from but for the first time I felt a thread of life in the story. I have long thought that blacks are going to have to lead this country out of the dead end of violence and retribution because they, perhaps more than any other Americans, have endured when deprived of power, have persevered when deprived of rights, and have grown in stature and grace when others tried to deny them dignity. It is presumptuous of me to tell their story, but perhaps no more presumptuous than writing from the point of view of a teenage girl who suffers a charming and beautiful sister or a middle-aged widow who for the first time in a long life must face living alone.

"Living with the Hyenas" began when an elderly aunt told me she had been at the cemetery cleaning my uncle's grave and saw a man she believed to be a lifelong friend cleaning his wife's grave. Her eyesight wasn't so good any more and she wasn't sure who it was so she didn't speak to him. Her lack of curiosity disturbed me because of the possibilities.

Also, I was intrigued by the idea of a romance beginning in a cemetery. The first time I wrote the story it became "The Midnight Clear." A woman burying her father meets a man burying his wife. They both need someone to care for and out of that need decide to marry. Love, if it comes, will come later.

I liked that story so I'm not sure why I went back to the cemetery for another romance, but I think it's because I wanted to explore middle-aged romance where the hormones don't overpower the heart. What happened was that the head overpowered the hormones. The story was first called "A Last Love," and Phloreene, while mourning her husband, finds a new love. I intended her first husband to be a compassionate and caring man but he didn't turn out that way. I thought the story would then become that of an ill-used woman who in her later years finds true love. No matter how I wrote the story, Maynard, the man she meets in the cemetery, became as self-important and selfish as her first husband. I tried to get her to marry him and return to the kind of marital yoke she had borne before but Phloreene was more level-headed than that. She was lonely and afraid but she was going to take a chance.

"A Boy and His Dog" is largely based on an incident I witnessed in Vietnam. The dog handler was walking point on a mixed patrol of Vietnamese and Americans when the dog became inattentive and missed some mines and trip wires. Most of the mines were crudely made and failed, but one exploded, critically wounding two Vietnamese. The handler was severely shaken and lost all confidence in the dog. I liked the idea of mutual trust and dependence, a theme that runs through several of the stories, but in this case the betrayer, the dog, is innocent of evil intent or even self-interest. The man, who is not innocent because he knows what he is doing, must betray the dog to save his life and limbs. The Vietnam setting was an accident, of course, but it added implications of the Garden of Eden with its tree of the knowledge of good and evil, the quality that differentiates the man from the dog.

"A Second Chance" was an attempt to answer the age-old problem of "Why does God permit evil?" which usually means, why does God permit me or someone I love to die? In the Old Testament, God added years to King Hezekiah's life. Was Hezekiah grateful? In the New Testament, Jesus raised Lazarus from the dead. Was Lazarus grateful? If I had the chance to add years to my life how many years would I want? Under what conditions and with what guarantees? It's a story that I've mentally toyed with for many years but first put to paper only two years ago.

"Reluctant Truth" is one of my earliest stories. Many years ago, I overheard a student say, "Thank God, I'm not like my sister." I was intrigued by the possibilities. What was he like and how was he different from his sister? I attempted the story many times without much success. The story was not funny until it became two sisters. After that I had the characters and most of the incidents in the story but I couldn't get the tone and voice right until I let Norma tell her story.

"How I Won the War" began when a rancher friend told me he once bought a dying horse. This was a story that didn't strike fire until I found the right time, World War II, and the boy has to decide between two right choices, his obligation as a human being and his obligation as a patriot.

"Fraternities" began in an early draft of the novel, *The Last Klick*, when one character told another character that one day an American and a Frenchman, neither of whom understood the language of the other, would have an intimate and heartfelt conversation in which the only words were Vietnam place-names accompanied by grunts and gestures. "Kontum." "Um." I tried to write it that way but I think it will work only on stage or on film and only for a short period of time. I had to flesh out the setting and the characters, but I still think the dialogue comes close to quintessential male intimacy.

"Women Don't Know" is another attempt to examine the difference between male and female relationships. The narrator thinks he knows Doc and he knows none of the things Doc's wife knows. The title could have as easily been "Men Don't Know," but not from the narrator's point of view. It could as easily have been set in a workplace where men work beside each other for years and never discover details that women discuss the first time they meet. I set it at a hunting camp because at play men come no closer to intimacy than they do at work.

"Defender of the Faith" is another of those stories that began when I first started writing. It is based on the shock I felt when I first discovered a school girl had been sexually intimate. I tried to write that story many times from the point of view of a young boy in love with an older girl. Later, it became the story of an old, embittered bachelor talking about the love he lost as a boy. Slowly, the reader was to realize that it was not Joy McKinney he loved but the idea of her purity. That led to thinking about how intensely children hold on to ill-defined abstract concepts like love, patriotism, success and sometimes never think beyond them. Nothing worked until Vietnam entered the story.

"Volunteers" began as a Vietnam story. Much of my writing about Vietnam has been prompted by the conviction that most Americans know nothing about Vietnam, which is okay, but think they know, which isn't okay. One of the reasons Vietnam veterans don't talk to outsiders about the war is because their memories are corrected by people who weren't there. "It wasn't like that," say those whose knowledge comes from Rambo movies and what television calls news. "Volunteers" is an encounter between an expert, cloaked in the certitude of book-learning, and a man who is confused because what he has experienced does not coincide with what he has learned. The women are counterpoint to the theme.

"Flight to Amman" grew out of an experience in which my wife and I were stranded, without visas, in a country where we could not speak the language or read the signs, and were not permitted to change money, make a telephone call or leave the terminal. It was the only time I remember feeling completely powerless with no control over my destiny. It's also the first time I understood some people's fear of flying. I've always loved flying and have a private pilot's license and had never understood how others fear surrendering control to a pilot. I wanted the reader to feel the alienation, almost an out-of-body experience of being a spectator to your own powerlessness. The alienated traveler seizes the only power left, that over fellow travelers.

"At Play in the Sewers of the Lord" began when a minister friend complained about the problems he had selling the sewage plant his father left him. Until that time I thought only municipalities owned sewage plants. The minister didn't appreciate my laughter at his problems, but there seemed something innately funny about a man temperamentally and educationally equipped for spiritual matters having to deal with the coarser elements of human existence. The only problem I had with the story was researching sewage treatment, which was not, otherwise, of great interest to me.

In some book or story, I can't remember where, I wrote "That's something I always knew but no one told me." I liked the line and it seemed to have implications beyond whatever its location was at that time; there are a lot of things we know or should know, although no one tells us. In effect, "Things No One Told Me" grew out of its own title. I wanted to illustrate the title with things I learned without being told. I suppose I set it in a country school because my earliest learning came in a country school and there was a boy like

Sidney and a teacher like Miss Codd, who also appears in *Wanderer Springs*.

At a meeting, I think in Abilene, I heard Liz Carpenter tell a story about her husband bringing home a statue of Jesus that for some reason was inappropriate. "But you can't take Jesus back," she said. I told her I was going to steal that story and she said I could have it. Unlike most of my stories that develop slowly on paper or in the computer, I developed this one on the drive back from Abilene and subsequent long drives over the next few months. Why was the gift inappropriate? Who would buy an inappropriate gift? How do you get rid of an inappropriate gift? The character and plot grew out of those questions. Finally, the question became, how do you turn something unfit into something felicitous? Transform dross into gold? A sow's ear into a silk purse?

The same kind of process was at work in "Games Children Play." A friend told me of a neighbor who refused to come outside for her own birthday party. Why? Who would give such a party? Grown children. Why would their mother refuse to come outside to her party? They embarrassed her by setting up garish tables and chairs on her lawn and by acting like little children. It was a funny idea, but when I wrote the story it was sad. The mother was pitiful, the children unlikable, selfish and sometimes vicious. I had the plot a long time before I had the tone or characters for this story. I had to assure the reader early in the story that it was okay to laugh at the children and okay to laugh at Rose; nothing bad was going to happen to them.

I suppose since I'm analyzing the process these stories went through, I should also analyze why I am getting around to "X-Mas" last. I've always had a love-hate relationship with Christmas. There is too much tinsel, glitter and sentimentality. Baby Jesus has never been as interesting to me as Jesus on the mount, in Gethsemane or on the road to Emmaus. My favorite holiday is Easter. It has also been commercialized, but no other day approaches the glory of Easter morning.

Some years ago I went to Israel to see Israel, not the Holy Land. Of course, it's impossible to avoid the Holy Land in Israel. Israel was intriguing. The Holy Land was annoying. Every place I wanted to see was covered by some monstrosity that was supposed to give reverence to the place. Abraham Lincoln said it more than a hundred years ago, "We cannot dedicate — we cannot consecrate — we cannot hallow — this ground." Those "who struggled here, have consecrated it far above our poor power to add or detract." I did think the buildings over holy places detracted from them. I had rather see a manger, a stable or even a replica of them than see some building supposedly constructed to consecrate the spot.

In "X-Mas" I wanted to find my way back to the simplicity of the gospel stories of shepherds and sheep and mangers that I've always loved. I wanted to find the likeness of Mary and Joseph in every person for whom the world has no place, the spirit of God in the birth of every child. Of course, I would be pleased if the reader found the spirit of God in every story, but I don't expect miracles. I only attest to them.

War

Land of the Free

Clarence lay sleepless, staring at the high ceiling of the old farmhouse. Fearing he had been deserted by those he thought he could trust, by those he had fought to save. He had known that fear before. Korea. Frozen Chosin. Surrounded. Fighting to keep the enemy off the ridges so the regiment could escape. He had been wounded in a running battle as the patrol pulled back to avoid being cut off.

He had fallen into a depression in the snow, so tired he wanted to sleep forever, so cold he couldn't imagine ever being warm. Stronger than the cold and the pain was the fear: he had been deserted, left behind. Then he heard them, Jeff, Green, Dixie. Marines did not leave buddies behind.

This time was different. He was surrounded again, but this time his countrymen were the enemy. He had been betrayed by their promise and his dream. Jeff who had saved him in Korea had betrayed him in Texas. But Jeff didn't ask him to come to Texas; not exactly. The decision had been his. All the decisions had been his. Did that mean he had betrayed himself? his daughter Venitia's happiness? her future?

That was most frightening of all. That he had been wrong all along. That he couldn't tell promises from lies, hope from self-deception. That was what made him sleepless: he had fooled himself. He had allowed himself to be deceived.

When Jeff had tracked him down after all those years, something had awakened in him, a comradeship, a brotherhood he had almost forgotten. The feeling he had as they hobbled down the road to live or die together. When they had been picked up by a patrol, they had put their heads together and cried. They had embraced, closer than brothers, exchanging an unspoken pledge of friendship forever. How could he not have responded to Jeff's call?

Jeff didn't exactly ask him to come to Texas, just as Jeff didn't exactly search for him because Jeff was dying. Jeff didn't even know he was dying, just that his condition was serious and he was getting around to doing things he should have done long ago. Besides, Clarence knew that he should have been the one doing the searching. After all, Jeff had carried him.

That wasn't the way Venitia had seen it. She didn't understand why he had to leave his job, his home, why she had to leave her school, her friends to go to some podunk place. She was going to high school the next year, be on the basketball team. "Why yo' his houseboy?" she asked. "Let one of his honky friends take care of him." He had explained that the regiment had been surrounded by waves of Chinese troops, that his buddies could have left him and caught up with the regiment but they had carried him, hiding when they could, fighting when they had to, but they had carried him.

Over that ridge or the next ridge or some ridge was the regiment. If they could reach the regiment they had a chance. Maybe Green and Dixie would still be alive if they hadn't tried to save him. Jeff was hobbling on frozen feet. "Go on," Clarence told him. "Save yourself."

"Don't quit on me; you're all I got," Jeff said.

"I'm not a quitter," Clarence told him.

They struggled over ridges, hiding, traveling at night. They reached the road and saw tank and tire marks in the snow; the regiment had already passed. For a moment he had given up. "Go on," he told Jeff again. "You can catch up by yourself."

"I can't make it alone," Jeff said.

"Yo shouldn't a been fighting a white man's war anyhow," Venitia said. "Yo' should a said, 'See ya, don't wanna be ya. Ain't nothing in it for folks like me-a.' "

"We're just going to see how Jeff is doing," he had told Venitia, but he knew better. He had wanted to make a change since Louise had died, wanted to get out of the inner city, wanted to get Venitia out, and he thought Jeff offered him a chance to do it. Venitia knew too much of hate, of anger. In some ways her mother's death had been harder on her than on him. "Sickle cell anemia," the doctor said. "Mostly affects black people." Even nature was prejudiced. "Nothing we could do," the doctor said. Clarence didn't like "nothing we could do." There was always something you could do.

As a single parent he had failed Venitia. Being shop foreman meant pride and success and responsibility. It also meant he wasn't home when she got there. He couldn't visit her school, volunteer as a PTA parent, talk to her teachers, meet her friends. When she got sick at school he had to call a former baby-sitter to get her and take her home. Texas would offer them a simpler life, he had thought. New friends, a chance to start over. This was America.

"All America means to me is bluebirds in badges sayin' 'keep moving, niggah, before I bust yo' ass.' "

"It's not perfect but it's still the best country in the world," he always told her.

"Yeah? Then why all them riots and marches?"

He was proud she believed black was beautiful, but she called white people "peckerwoods," called those in authority "pigs," wore clothes that his mother and her mother would have been ashamed to wear, used words at home that he used only in the shop, and talked street talk, refusing to speak the way she was taught at school and at home. He worked hard to speak proper English so that no one could call him ignorant or low-class. Venitia called it citizen English, gray grammar.

Venitia was almost arrested for protesting the Vietnam war. Clarence was confused about the war but he knew the Marines were there and he was not. When he referred to brother Marines she pretended he was talking about black Marines and said they were drafted so white meat could stay in school. He told her Marines were volunteers, something she knew. She said they volunteered because they couldn't get jobs or they were learning skills to fight the revolution.

Talk of revolution disturbed him. His father had tried to join the Marines after Pearl Harbor but there were no black Marines then. His father had dreamed of being a shop foreman but had been a Tuskeegee pilot, shot down while escorting a crippled bomber. Clarence had been what his father had dreamed and Venitia had chances he had never had. It was a frustrating evolution, so slow that families were torn apart by dreams and broken hearts, lives burned up in rage and expectations. Venitia refused to see movement at all. When he pointed it out, she called him an oreo. That's when he knew he had to leave. Jeff's call was just the excuse.

"Yo' don' know them crackers," she told him, harboring some instinctive fear of white strangers. "Yo' don' know what they like."

"They're Americans, just like us, whether they live in the North or the South," he had lied. When he was a boy, his mother had wanted to visit his father's camp in Alabama but his father said no, things were bad in the South. Blacks couldn't go to movies, bars, restaurants, not even blacks in uniform; black officers couldn't go to white officers' clubs.

Clarence had been in Marine boot camp with southerners who gave Rebel yells, waved the Confederate flag, said "niggah." He had to fight for his place, but in Korea he was a Marine and they wouldn't have deserted him no matter what color he was because Marines didn't leave their wounded. They went by the rules and folks would do that in Texas too. Besides, "I know Jeff — he's my friend."

"Maybe he be the best of 'em, maybe he the only one like him, and he some friend askin' yo' to give up yo' home and job and go and heed him."

"He didn't ask me. I see the need. That's all. I see the need."

"Maybe yo' his bond servant but I ain't gon' be. I ain't gon' be bound to nothin' or nobody."

He hadn't expected the move to be so difficult for her. Jeff said he had a couple of hundred acres in the country; Venitia could have a dog, a cat, her own horse if she wanted one. If she fed the hens, she could sell the eggs. She could never have had those things in Detroit, but when he told her, Venitia said he wouldn't get her a horse when she had wanted one and now she didn't want a horse, she wanted a car. She wanted to stay where she was, although since her mother died she had hated the house, hated the neighborhood, hated school, hated Detroit.

He had thought she was afraid of a new place, a new life, and had explained that learning to live with fear was a sign of maturity. He didn't admit that he was afraid himself, a little. He hadn't seen Jeff in fifteen years. He had often thought he should find Jeff and had intended to do so, but Jeff was white and Clarence had procrastinated. He wasn't sure how a white homeboy would respond to a long-ago black friend. Clarence had always had to prove himself; would he have to prove himself again?

When Jeff had called, Clarence had been pleased that the ties they had established on the road to Hagaru-ri were still there and color wasn't. He had agreed to come to Texas. Nevertheless, he had been afraid that he wouldn't know Jeff anymore, that Jeff wouldn't know him, that after a couple of hours of talking old times they'd have nothing to say, that he would fail Jeff, that Jeff would be a disappointment to him.

He promised himself if he and Venitia weren't comfortable after a week, they would move on to Arizona or California. He had the money from sale of the house, Louise's life insurance, his savings, and he was a skilled mechanic. He could get a job anywhere. He hadn't explained that to Venitia because he didn't want his fears to exacerbate her own.

He had taken Venitia to Texas, to a little dried-up place a few miles from a little dried-up town. "Welcome home," Jeff said. Jeff was older, grayer, but he still had that wide Texas grin and hugging, back-slapping openness that not even Venitia could resist. With a pride that was infectious he limped around showing them his "place," the solid frame house with the big yard, good barn, garden, henhouse, pasture with a few cows and an old mare he hoped would win Venitia's heart. He loved the place with its memories and personal imprints, like the bathroom on the porch.

"Granddad wouldn't have a toilet in the house, said it wasn't fitting, and no amount of reasoning could change his mind, even when he couldn't make it to the outhouse by himself. After he died, Dad built a bathroom on the porch."

Venitia was surprised to discover the little graveyard where Jeff's mother, father and grandparents were buried. "They're part of this place," Jeff explained. "Always will be. I want to be buried here too."

Clarence hadn't thought much about Jeff's wish at the time and didn't pay much attention when Jeff scarcely touched his food. He thought it was the excitement of the reunion. When Jeff continued to resist food, he asked about it. "Don't have any appetite," Jeff said. "I try to eat but I just can't." He laughed at his stubbornness.

Clarence laughed with him. One of the things he had liked about Jeff was his quiet strength. Jeff had been even thinner when the two of them hobbled along, leaning on each other, on the frozen road to Hagaru-ri. "We won't ever have to live this day again," Jeff had said to encourage them. "That's another mile we won't have to walk again."

Before the week was up, Clarence's fears were over and so were his thoughts of moving on. Jeff didn't talk about the war. He talked about his place, his grandparents who homesteaded it, his parents who hung on to it. "I joined the Marines to get away from this. Over there, it's what I missed the most. Being part of something. Being connected. It's what kept me going down that road. I want you and Venitia to feel what I felt."

Clarence didn't mention the conversation to Venitia. She would hear being connected as being bound.

Jeff had a lot of things in need of repair, including a baler, a tractor that needed an overhaul and a truck so long disused that the engine had frozen. "I don't know nothing about farming but this equipment is worn out," Clarence said.

"Don't have a lot of use for it anymore," Jeff said. "I been selling off the place a few acres at a time to keep going. To a neighbor, Royce Harmon. His family has been here as long as my family, and his son, Pie, wants to be a farmer, but Royce knows the days of the small family farm are gone and he has to grow or go. He can only afford a few acres at a time and that's all I'm willing to sell."

Jeff shook his head. "Down to my last two hundred acres but I won't sell that no matter what. I got to have some place to be buried in." He laughed and Clarence tried to laugh with him. "I got to have something to leave behind."

"What happened to that girl you talked about all the time? Eileen?"

"She waited until I got home. I give her credit for that. But back here, it didn't look the way I saw it over there. Everything seemed so mean. Small. Most people don't look any farther than the end of their field. A high school football game is the biggest thing that ever happens. They're good people but they're limited. Self-limited."

"Is that the same as being connected?"

"Connections should make you bigger. This place can be a foundation or a graveyard. That's one of the 'modern' notions folks said I came home with. They said Korea had changed me. I guess it did. Eileen and I didn't have much in common anymore."

"There's got to be more than one woman here."

"If they don't get engaged in high school, they leave to get a job or go to college. I went with one woman when she was home from college but she found a law student she liked better. A divorcee said she saw potential in the place but it would take too much work. Was engaged to a woman from Dallas. She lived here for a while but it was too backward, like being at a family reunion where everybody was trying to win Grandpa's favor by making everyone else look bad. I almost sold the place and moved to Dallas with her. Then I thought about Mom and Dad and Granddad and I couldn't do it.

"Course I've been selling it off a piece at a time but I kept some for them. Then I had to figure out what to do with it. I could sell it to Royce but it wouldn't mean as much to him as what his daddy left him. I could leave it to the church but they'd sell it to the highest bidder. I got to thinking about the way I felt about the place over there in Korea. The kind of vision I had, with everybody doing their best and not leaving anybody behind. I thought of how we saved each other. I should've called you a long time ago."

"I could have called," Clarence said.

"When I go, this is yours. That's why I started looking for you; I was making a will. I'd like for you to stay, but that's not why I invited you to come. I didn't want you to sell it before you had a chance to see it the way I see it."

"If any of it's mine, I'm selling and moving on," Venitia told Clarence after her first day at school. Both he and Venitia were startled to find that integration had not come to this part of the United States, not this school district.

"Not never," said a black neighbor who came by to take Venitia to school because there were no buses for blacks. "They ain't never gon' integrate this place. They don' believe in no Supreme Court no more than they believe in Brother King."

"I wanna go home," Venitia said.

In Detroit she wanted nothing to do with whites. In Texas, she didn't want to go to an all-black school. "They ain't even got textbooks for ever'body," she said. The textbooks they had were out of date; they had no workbooks, maps, charts, science equipment, library or periodicals. Worksheets and exams were copied on an old hectograph like they had when he was a boy, before someone invented the mimeograph machine. Next year she would be going to high school and there was no high school for blacks.

He promised to get her in the high school or they would leave. "We'll try Arizona or California," he said.

"I don' want to stop in California," she said. "I want to move clean on out of this mess. I don' want no more America."

"You find a better place and I'll consider it," he said.

She was mollified until she discovered that none of her friends was going to high school, even if they could get in. What was the use? Nobody was going to hire them to work in an office or a store. Most of them did seasonal farm work when they could get it. Mr. Scott at the grain elevator-cotton compress-fertilizer plant hired them as soon as they were able to work, paid minimum wage too, so if he offered a job they dropped out of school to take it because there might not be another chance.

When Venitia told them her father had been a shop foreman, that he had white men working under him, they ducked their heads and chuckled. "Girl, y'all done come to the wrong place."

"Don't any of them want to go to high school?" he had asked her.

"They 'fraid they folks be fired or mugged if they try. These blacks is diff'ent. They whupped. I told 'em they need ta go ta Detroit or some place. They said this was they home."

"See, it can't be as bad as you think," he told her, refusing to lapse into the dialect she affected. "This is their home,too. This is still America."

"Yo' right. This is sho' 'nuff America. There ain't no school, there ain't no jobs, there ain't no place for us."

"Then why do they stay, Venitia? Because there are people here who see a future for themselves and their children."

"Yo' right. At school, for an example the teachers all talk 'bout Homer, janitor over at the white-bread school. He got a regular job, workin' inside when it's cold and rainy outside. School give 'im a turkey ever Christmas. Ain't that nice? They treat him bettah than a dog."

"You're going to high school next year," he promised her, as he had promised her mother. "And you're going to college." Her mother's life insurance would take care of that no matter what happened to him.

"Yo' gon' get in trouble," she said.

"Y'all gon' git in big trouble," said the minister at the black church they attended. He was a little man, his face shiny and fringed with white, not educated but wise to sin and doubt. "Some of us lived heah and fought dis fight all our lives. Y'all newcomers and when trouble start for ever'body, even our folks gon' say y'all should'a done stayed where y'all come from."

Jeff had said they could go to church with him and he

would take on anyone who complained, including the preacher. Jeff couldn't take on lunch, much less a church full of white Christians.

"The most dangerous thang on earth for black folks is white Christians," the black minister said. "Y'all threatenin' they way of life. They believe in segregation and Robert E. Lee same as they believe in Jesus and George Washington. I'll help y'all all I can but y'all best know right now, y'all not just askin' 'em to change they minds. Y'all askin' 'em to change they lives, to put old massuh in his grave."

"This is America," Clarence told the school superintendent. "It's the law of the land."

"Folks here are as fine and law-abiding as folks anywhere," the superintendent told him. "But I don't want to do something that will hurt the school and damage community feelings and you don't want to do anything that will bring harm to you or your daughter."

Clarence threatened to call the NAACP, the White House, to speak to Lyndon Johnson personally. The superintendent dropped the pose. "I can't stop her from coming to school but there are people who can and will. I want you to go home and think about that. I want you to look at your little girl and explain to her what happens to people who think their opinion is better than that of everyone else in the community."

He didn't tell Venitia, and he didn't tell Jeff. Jeff's condition had been diagnosed as pancreatic cancer, and Clarence was driving him to the doctor's office for his appointments, to the hospital for his treatments, tending Jeff's garden and livestock and repairing the machinery that had been brought to him.

Jeff had told everyone that Clarence was a skilled mechanic. Farmers dropped off electric motors or picked him up to repair their tractor, truck, combine. Royce Harmon had been the first. The Harmons lived on a farm a few miles down the road. Royce's truck had broken down on the way to town and he had walked to Jeff's place for help. Clarence had taken a look at the truck, cleaned the carburetor and gotten it running, but he told Royce the truck needed a new carburetor, fuel pump and generator. He told Royce he would replace them if Royce got the parts. Royce thanked him without offering to pay and ignored his advice until the truck broke down again.

"I'll tell you something about Royce," Jeff told Clarence. "I got sick and got behind and Royce came over every day to milk the cows, feed the hens, pick up the eggs and plant the garden. He's prejudiced like everybody around here but he's a good neighbor. He don't want to give up being better than others but he don't want to give up being good neither."

"I need your niggah to do some work on my truck," Royce told Jeff the next week.

"Clarence is my friend," Jeff told him. "If you need his help talk to him."

"Jeff lost something over there in that Korea," Royce said after Jeff walked away. "It wasn't just his toes neither. He lost his pride. Sense of who he is."

"Who is he?" Clarence asked.

"One of us. Least he used to be. Now he don't know who he is. Being an American don't seem to mean anything to him anymore."

"What does it mean to you?"

"It means being the best . . . strongest . . . MacArthur would have let you boys finish the job over there. With atom bombs if necessary."

"MacArthur almost got us killed. And what was America when it wasn't the strongest?"

"I don't have time to waste talking to you. How much you going to charge me for fixing my truck?" When Clarence told Royce how much the work would cost, Royce said, "They'll do it in town for that much."

"They won't do it as well," Clarence said.

"You better hope your hands can live up to your mouth, niggah."

"My name is Clarence, and you're free to take your truck anywhere you want. But if you want the best you'll bring it to me. And if you don't agree I'm the best, you're free to tell everybody that I'm no better than those white mechanics in town. That's what being an American means."

"I'll not only tell everybody what a big-mouthed, sorry-ass niggah you are, if you don't fix my truck right, I'm not going to pay you."

"Sounds fair," Clarence said.

Royce thought that over for a moment. "I'll bring the truck tomorrow. Might as well overhaul it while you got it," he said.

The next day Royce brought the truck. His son, Pie, came to pick him up. Pie was a big, freckled, red-headed high-school kid. Clarence spoke to him, expecting the son to be a little ashamed of the backwardness of his father, but he was wrong.

"Pa, you ought to let me fix that. I can do anything a damn niggah can do," Pie swaggered. "And do it better."

"You just get yourself ready for football to start," Royce said. "That's what I want you to do."

"We gonna be a better team this year," Pie said, shouldering Clarence aside when they left.

"I thought the younger ones would be more broad-minded," Clarence said.

"They're scared." Jaeff replied. "This whole way of life is disappearing. Their folks walked a hard road and the road keeps getting steeper. They don't know what's going to happen to them."

"Nobody knows what's going to happen to them," Clarence said. "That's why we have to rely on each other."

"Pic thinks he's something special because he's on the football team," Jeff said. "But he's not very good. None of them are. There are some black boys that could help them but Pie and his friends don't want any blacks playing with them. And they sure don't want to play against any. They've never had to compete with blacks and the idea that a black could be better is something they can't face."

"Had they rather lose?"

"This is the South. We kinda turned lost causes into a religion. Appomattox was our Calvary. But the South is going to rise again to save the nation and lead it back to the truth."

"What truth is that?"

"God over man, man over woman, white over black and the chosen look after decent women and other folks who need protection from temptation and those who would corrupt them."

"I think I want to be chosen," Clarence said.

"Too late for you and me. God has already told them who needs protecting and who's going to do the protecting, and would you believe God didn't say nothing to those who needed protecting?"

"Sounds to me like God is prejudiced."

"Brother Clarence, you done memorized the creed."

⁂

Clarence didn't have the space or the tools he needed to fix Royce's truck, but he rigged a garage in the barn, bought some used tools and went to work surrounded by the history of Jeff's family. Both Jeff's father and grandfather had kept records in pencil on the barn walls. Dates of the first bale of cotton each year, when they planted corn, wheat, alfalfa, when they harvested, when cows came fresh, when they changed the oil on the truck or tractor.

Each day Clarence made his way to the barn through a graveyard of outdated cultivators and seeders, past a shop containing a forge and anvil for shaping horse and mule shoes, and worked amid a museum of mule harness, rolls of rusted barbed wire, old clocks and radios, dusty saws and windmill parts. Each day Royce stopped by to check on him. The last day, Clarence said, "Crank it up and let's see how it sounds."

Royce started the engine, raised the hood to look inside, took the truck for a test drive and then went to get Pie to take his car home. “Sounds okay,” Royce said. “I’ll know in a week or two. If it runs okay I’ll pay you what you wanted. If it doesn’t I’ll tell everybody in the county there’s a no ’count niggah over here who thinks he’s a mechanic.”

Clarence had customers and a reputation as the best mechanic in a hundred miles when Jeff died.

Jeff had explained that he and Clarence had been buddies in Korea, had saved each other’s lives and that Clarence had come to visit and had stayed to help him. Nevertheless, people thought Venitia was Jeff’s cook and housekeeper and Clarence his chauffeur, handyman and mechanic.

When Jeff’s condition worsened, Royce came to buy the farm. “It’s about your place,” Royce said to Jeff, waiting for Clarence to be dismissed. When Jeff didn’t send Clarence out of the room, Royce continued. “I want to buy it, what’s left of it.”

“I’m leaving it to Clarence,” Jeff said.

“Come again,” Royce said in shock. “What’s he gonna do with it?”

“Whatever he wants.”

“He can’t make a living off two hundred acres. Nobody can.”

“He doesn’t have to. Clarence is the best mechanic around. This will be his home if he wants to stay.”

“Niggahs don’t have no place here.”

“Clarence has this one. He’s my friend and he’s my heir.”

“You sold me the rest of it. What’s so special about this part?”

“I was born here. I’m going to be buried here.”

“I’m not going to plow up your grave or your folks’ either.”

“I know that, Royce. But you’ll sell the house and plow up the yard. You’ll move the barn and let the shop fall down.”

“I can’t believe you’re doing this. As long as we been neighbors.”

"Royce, you want to buy this place and leave it to Pie. I understand that. Why can't you understand I want to leave it to Clarence?"

"I can't believe you're giving it to a niggah instead of selling it to me. I don't know what he's holding over you, but I don't like it."

"Me and him are bound to each other, Royce. We saved each other. My place is his place and he can do anything he wants to with it when I'm gone because he's got the right. He's my heir."

"Folks are not going to like this," Royce said. "I don't know what happened to you over there in Korea but I don't like it one bit."

"What happened to you Royce?"

"My folks needed me to help with the farm. I'm not no draft dodger."

"That was a long time ago. What has happened to you since?"

"Nothing."

"That's what I'm talking about, Royce. You're being left behind — you, the school, the town. The world is going on without you."

"Let them go. I never cared much for the rest of the world anyway."

"And Pie? You want him left behind? You want to leave your grandkids at the mercy of those who did keep up? You have a chance to make a difference."

"I don't want anything different and neither does anybody else around here. There's too much different already."

"Royce, my daddy and your daddy didn't want them running natural gas lines under their farms. They didn't want high lines across their fields. Now we have gas stoves, electric lights, television. We had to be dragged into the twentieth century, but now we're glad to be here."

"We'll see about that," Royce said, leaving without a goodbye.

"I told them," Jeff said. "I told all of them. They don't want to accept it but they will."

Clarence understood. Property was a white man's establishment. It was his identity, his security. If they could deny him and Venitia a place, then they could deny their permanence. Without the place Jeff left them, he and Venitia would be as invisible as the other blacks who owned nothing but the land the church stood on.

When Clarence took Jeff to the hospital for the last time, Jeff said, "Don't quit on me; I can't make it alone."

"I'll stay right beside you," Clarence promised, but they wouldn't let him in Jeff's room. "You go on home. We'll call you when it's time to come get him."

He and Venitia stood outside the church at Jeff's funeral. At the graveyard behind the house, they stood apart from the other mourners, mostly neighbors. Royce and his wife were there, Pie with them. Clarence and Venitia waited until everyone left — no one spoke to them — then said a prayer at Jeff's grave.

When people learned Jeff had left the farm to Clarence, even Clarence's customers turned against him. They believed he took advantage of Jeff's illness and tricked him into changing his will. No matter that he showed them the will, dated before he and Venitia had come to Texas; they refused to believe. Jeff's car was confiscated because he still owed money on it, and the dealer refused to let Clarence pay for it, saying he was paying with Jeff's money that he had no right to. The bank demanded immediate repayment of a loan that Jeff had gotten to pay his medical expenses, and Clarence had to break his vow to Louise in order to pay it with her insurance money.

Even worse, he had no income because his customers no longer came. He and Venitia had milk and butter, vegetables from Jeff's garden and the eggs that Venitia had been selling because now she had no way to get to town and none of the white neighbors would buy from her. When there were no vegetables, they ate eggs.

One night, Royce Harmon came. His well pump had failed and if he didn't get water soon he would lose cattle. Clarence repaired the pump. Royce not only paid him, he bought eggs. "Might as well make it two dozen. May be a while before I get to town," Royce said.

After that, others came, always emergencies, always after dark. He was working again, Venitia was selling a few eggs, they had money for clothes and groceries. Then he told the school superintendent his daughter was going to the all-white high school and no one came. Not even after dark.

Venitia wanted him to sell the farm and go someplace else, anywhere else, but he refused. He couldn't explain why to Venitia because he wasn't sure why. If he had received a decent offer, he might have sold but the same people who accused him of gaining the land by trickery tried to buy it below market value by threat. That was too much like running away.

He knew how much the land meant to Jeff, but this was his land now. He had already started his own record-keeping on the walls of the old barn and his own museum of starters, generators, alternators, motors, airconditioners that he thought someday he could use or repair. This was his home and no one was going to run him off. That was the black pride Venitia talked about.

He had seen the family cemetery behind the house, he had buried Jeff beside his parents, grandparents. Clarence's father was buried in a military cemetery in Belgium, his mother in Detroit, one set of grandparents was lost someplace in Georgia, another grandfather in St. Louis and grandmother in Cincinnati. He didn't know if his ancestors had been slaves. Sometimes he hoped they had been, that he shared that with his brothers. Sometimes he hoped they hadn't, that his people had always been free. He wanted Venitia to know more of her ancestors than that. He wanted her to come from people who bore their burdens with strength and pride and earned their freedom with courage and humility. Who left records of their passage. He wanted her to have a place.

Sending Venitia to that white school was the hardest thing he had ever done. Harder than trying to catch the regiment fighting its way to the sea. He felt helpless and it wasn't a feeling he was comfortable with. He wanted to go to school with her, force them to accept her but he had no car and she was safer — because less threatening — alone than accompanied by a male. She was braver than he had ever been, braver than he could imagine anyone being.

"I'm gon' be lynched," she said.

He assured her that no one would harm her but that some might insult her. "Just consider the kind of people they are."

"Yeah, white people."

"Didn't you like Jeff? Wasn't he fair with you?"

"He asked yo' to give up yo' job, give up yo' home, me to give up my school and friends so yo' could come down here and be his houseboy."

"He needed me."

"He needed somebody; it didn't have to be yo'."

"We were friends."

"I had friends, I went to a good school, but I had to leave that and come down here where folk hate me before they know who I am. They want to kill me 'cause I'm gon' be in the same room with they kids."

He had no answer to that except that the people she had to face were not her enemies, they were Americans, they were Christians and no matter what they said, they would live by the laws of their God and country.

He wanted to believe that. Unable to sleep that night, he had alternated between praying that his fellow citizens would respect his daughter and swearing vengeance on anyone who harmed her. He had given her a couple of boiled eggs for lunch and sent her alone to walk the hundred yards or so to the county road where the school bus passed, while he pretended to work on the tractor.

The bus did not stop. He watched her return to the house humiliated. He tried to comfort her; the driver didn't understand. If the driver was educated he would be doing something beside driving a school bus. "They all crackers, white trash crackers," she said, biting her lip to keep it from trembling, anger, stubbornness and pride forcing tears to her eyes. "I hate 'em."

"The bus will stop for you tomorrow," he promised her and himself. She had rights, constitutional rights, and as a Marine he had taken an oath to defend the Constitution. "I don't care whether they like you or you like them, you are going to that school."

The next day he walked to the road with her and waved at the driver to stop. When the bus did not slow down, he stood in the middle of the dirt road. The driver turned on his lights, honked his horn, but Clarence did not budge. He was frightened but if he backed down now, Venitia would never go to school. The bus slid to a stop, blanketing him in dust. The driver yelled at him to get out of the way, the children screamed insults, but the bus door did not open.

"My daughter is going to school. She is riding that bus."

"We don't want her," the children screamed. "Zulu. Handkerchief head. Go back where you came from, Aunt Jemima. Stick with your own kind." The boys yelled worse insults at her color, her gender, her physical appearance. "I didn't know they made apes that tall." "That ain't no ape, that's an orangutan." "Don't she shine." "Looks like a Hershey bar wearing a Brillo pad."

"Get out of the road," the driver yelled through an open window.

"I'm not moving until she's on that bus," Clarence said. He could see Venitia trembling beside the bus door but she didn't back up and neither would he.

"Move before I run over you."

"I'm not moving."

"We don't want her."

"It's the law," he said. "She has a right."

The driver reluctantly opened the door. Without looking at him, Venitia got on the bus, walking through the taunts and insults to an empty seat. "Look out, don't let none of that black rub off on you." "Show us your blue gums, Sapphire." "Somebody spilled ink all over you, honey."

For a moment he almost told her to get off the bus; no one should have to endure those insults, that hatred. He wished a couple of those high-school boys would get off the bus and say something to him. He knew how to fight that kind of fight.

He had to summon up courage to let her go. He had walked out of frozen Chosin, the bravest thing he had ever done. But he hadn't been alone. He was sending Venitia into an ambush and she was going alone. He stepped out of the road, the door closed and the bus rolled away. He watched but Venitia did not look back.

He watched until the bus passed out of sight, ready to run to her side if they put her off the bus, if she called for help. Still he stood in the road, not knowing what to do. Should he walk to the school and tell them if they let her go unharmed he would take her home? No longer threaten their assumed superiority? They were his countrymen. They were Christians. They were his people and they would not harm his daughter.

He walked back to the house fighting tears at her courage. Getting on the bus. Going to a strange school, at the mercy of strangers. Not being able to count on the authorities to defend her rights. What kind of pride, what kind of courage did that require? Where did she get it? It had taken all the courage he had to let her go.

He tried to work on some of the broken machinery around the farm; if he could get it to working maybe he could sell it, but he couldn't concentrate on what his hands were doing. He thought of Venitia, imagining what she was going through. He waited for the bus to return her, wondering what he would do if she did not get off, where he could go for help. The bus slowed, stopped, Venitia got off with a load of books under her arms. He could hear shouts and laughter from the bus but he couldn't tell if they were directed at her.

He walked out to meet her but she shrugged past him. If she had been crying he couldn't tell it. He followed her to the house and asked how she liked school, but she said she had to fix dinner and then do her homework. "I got to learn a song for Glee Club. 'This land is my land, this land is your land,' " she said.

At dinner he asked if she made any friends. "They don' know nothin' outside football and cows. One of 'em thought Detroit was in the state of New York."

He asked what her teachers were like. "They do they job," she said. "They look at me like 'Who put this load of trouble in my room?' But if you took a snake in there they'd try to teach it something."

"Your grandmother wanted to be a teacher," he told her. "Before Dad was killed in the war. Maybe you can be a teacher."

"If they hired me, they'd have to pay me same as they pay them white teachers."

"Do you want to be a teacher?" he asked, wanting to be close to her, to chip away at the fear that isolated them from each other.

"I want to go where don' nobody know me and don' nobody care."

"Wasn't anyone nice to you?"

She shrugged. "Mr. Walker said he was glad to have me."

Something warm and syrupy surged through him. At least one teacher accepted her. "What does he teach?"

"He the coach."

"Did you tell him you play basketball?"

"They ain't got no team for girls." She paused to let him understand her disappointment. "He say I can try out for volleyball."

"Would you like to?"

She fidgeted in her chair. "Have to beat out one of the other girls. They all seniors. Played together three years."

It was a question. If she played she would change the dynamics of the team, force herself on them. He didn't know how good she was but he knew what it was like to replace someone popular. He had replaced a white foreman who was demoted after fifteen years. "You'll have to prove yourself," he warned. "They'll be watching every mistake."

They do that already. Shoot, I can outjump any of them lily pads."

She was going to try and he was glad, in a way. He wanted her to take over the team, to be the star, but he knew what it would cost her. How much easier it would be for her, and for him, if she sat quietly at the back of the room, did her work and never raised her hand. Nobody minded blacks as long as they were light, quiet and uptight.

After that, the bus always stopped for her, but short of the road or past where she stood so that she had to walk to the bus while the children taunted her. He told her to maintain her dignity, not stoop to their level and to tell the principal. The principal said they had to let her in the school and the bus had to pick her up, but he couldn't make the children like her. And as for the bus stopping exactly where she stood, he had more important things to deal with.

"Coach want me to ask for free lunch," she said one day. "He say all them eggs gonna make me roost. Cafeteria woman say free lunch be for white kids, they never had no black kid ask for one. I say, maybe that's 'cause there ain't never been no black kids here befo'. She say, 'Don' talk smart with me. That may work with Yankee charities but when yo' ask for help here yo' ask respectful and yo' act like yo' need it.' "

One day she brought home soap and shampoo and announced she was supposed to use it every day. "Boys have to milk cows ever' day 'fore school and they lean they heads on the cows' sides so they can dope off while they milking and they get lice. I told the teacher I don't have lice. Them white boys have lice. She sent me to the office for acting up."

The partial year at the segregated school had set Venitia back but she quickly caught up and made the A-B honor roll. She also made the volleyball team, displacing the captain and most popular girl in the school. He knew when she walked home from the school bus that something was wrong but he hadn't expected it to be success.

"I thought they was gon' like me," she said. "Then Coach named me to the team. Now they don' like me again."

"It's a change for them after playing together but they'll get used to it."

"If I don' play so well, let her have her position back, they'll like me better."

That was a tough call. He had been reluctant to replace a popular foreman but management said he had to think of what was best for the shop. "We all want to be liked, but who is the better player for the team? For the school?"

"I am, but they won't be no team. They won't set the ball for me."

"Would they rather lose without you or win with you?"

"They rather lose. I can't win by myself and if we lose ever'body is gon' blame me for mocusing the team."

At times like these he realized how much he needed Louise, how often he failed without her. "I guess you got to decide how you want them to accept you, because you're a better player or because you're willing to be second best to get along."

"That ain't no answer. Yo' a parent, yo' sposed to know what to do."

He didn't know what to do. He didn't even know if she did the right thing. He walked the four miles to town to see the first game, sat by himself at the top row of the gym, and watched them lose, although he thought they played well individually, Venitia better than anyone. He expected to walk home, but the coach, who had to take Venitia home, offered him a ride as well.

The coach was rumpled, ponderous and looked like his feet hurt. Clarence wondered how he had ever played volleyball or any sport. "The regular bus driver is going to have an operation," Mr. Walker said. "I'll recommend you for the job. I'll ask them to let you keep the bus at home and drive Venitia to the games and back. We don't want her missing any games."

"I'd keep the bus running good," Clarence promised. "And Venitia won't miss any games. I just hope we don't lose any more."

"They have to learn to play together," Mr. Walker said.

They had won the next game and lost the next. "They won't give me a chance," Venitia said.

"You play for the team, for the school," he advised her. "If they play for themselves everybody's going to know."

"They already know but they don' do nothin' about it."

Clarence had seen it happen since he was a child. Life, sometimes the whole country, honored the takers who looked out for no one but themselves. Still he didn't believe it. He hadn't wanted to spend his life as a Marine but they had taught him esprit de corps. There was a spirit bigger than the individual.

"My daddy, your grandfather, lost his life protecting a crippled bomber. He could have run off and saved himself but he didn't. He attacked three German fighters. The bomber crew wrote Mama about it."

"Yeah, and they went home to they pink wives and they offay jobs and Grandma had to work minimum wage to raise you."

One day Venitia didn't get off the bus. He was terrified.

He didn't have a telephone. He didn't have a car. Maybe she had missed the bus. Maybe there was extra practice after school and the coach was bringing her home. Should he look for her or should he wait for her? Twice he walked to the road, as though that would help, then walked back to the house to prepare dinner.

Unable to wait any longer he started walking to town and saw Venitia coming. He walked faster until he saw she was all right. She was tired, angry and discouraged. The bus driver was in the hospital for an operation and they hired one of the older students, Pie Harmon, to drive the bus. "They rather hire a white boy than you," she said.

"Why didn't you get off the bus?"

"I yelled at him to stop. He said, 'I thought you liked to ride the bus, niggah. Sit at the back where you belong.' "

Pie drove the bus back to school and when he stopped, he and his friends sat in the bus and made her walk through them. "You know what Martin Luther Coon is doing? He's marching. All the niggahs is marching, so you can get off the bus and march home."

"They didn't touch you?"

"They just said things."

"Venitia, did you do anything to give them an excuse to bother you?"

"I didn't do nothin'."

"Was this the first day for that boy to drive the bus?"

"He been driving most a week."

He realized she hadn't wanted to disappoint him by telling him they didn't want him as a driver. She didn't want to destroy his fragile faith in his country. "There must be some reason why he did it."

"Yeah, I'm black."

Then why didn't Pie refuse to stop the first day? Clarence finished preparing dinner while Venitia bathed.

"I'm too tired to eat," she said. "Or do homework or nothin'."

"You have to eat. Don't you have a game tomorrow?"

"Out of town. Means after school we be on the bus 'til time for the game. I ain't gon' be in no shape to play."

Suddenly he understood. "They think they can make you quit. Or that you'll be too tired to play your best. They're trying to break your spirit."

"They don' want me on they team. They don' want me representin' they school."

"It's not just their school, it's your school. The walk didn't hurt you. Insults can't stop you."

"They won't set me the ball. I don' want to ride the bus no more. I don' want to play for them."

He wanted to tell her she was playing for herself, but she was playing for them, otherwise team meant nothing. "You have to learn to trust them and to work together."

"What was yo' doing walking down the road?" she asked.

He was walking down the road because he didn't trust them either. "You go to the game tomorrow, you play the best you can and I'll talk to Pie Harmon."

"You gon' fight them boys and we gon' be lynched."

"I don't know what I'm going to do, but the bus is going to stop for you like any other rider."

The next day was Friday and the coach would be bringing her home after the game out of town. Clarence didn't have to worry about the bus stopping to let her off until Monday. Instead of spending one sleepless night, he had spent four, restless with fear that he had been deserted by those he had fought to save. Tormented with doubt that his country was the place he thought it was, was worth fighting for.

He had to stop the tormenting of his daughter because no one else would. They would make heroes of those who defeated her. But if he struck back they would strike back at him, and her. And who would come to their defense?

It was late when Venitia got home and she was exhausted. "We lost," she said slumping into a chair. "Coach say I play my best game, but we still lost. He say if the others don' keep up, he start some younger players and build a team 'round me." She placed her head in her arms and he thought she was going to cry. "If he do, we won't win another game and they gon' blame me for that too."

"But next year they'll be better and you'll be used to playing together."

She looked at him like next year was the worst thing that could happen to her. She didn't say, but he knew she wanted to leave. Go home. Go anywhere.

"Venitia, they're not vicious, they're just ignorant."

"They not as ig'nert as yo', thinkin' yo' could come here and be one of them. I don't wanna be one of them. I hate 'em. I hate this place. And I hate yo' for bringin' me here." She burst into tears and ran to her bedroom.

He knocked on her door but she wouldn't answer. "Venitia, may I come in?"

"I'm tryin' to sleep," she said.

He went to bed, but he couldn't sleep. He had put her in this situation and if he didn't do something, they might try even harder to drive her from the team. All he could think of was pounding their faces, teaching them what pain and humiliation felt like. But that was not only self-defeating, it would place her in greater danger. If he beat their kids, they would beat her and maybe do worse to him.

Saturday they went their own ways, she sleeping late, catching up on school work, reading, he working on the frozen engine, taking it apart piece by piece and examining the damage. It was a mess, the pistons rusty, the cylinders scarred, but if he could get the tolerances right he could save it, make it work again.

Sunday the church was full of eyes and they were all on him and Venitia. He didn't know how much they knew, but they knew he and Venitia had attracted the attention of the whole community. The church members always seemed to know what blacks the whites had targeted as troublemakers, and they watched him and Venitia with mixed hopes and fears, hoping they would show the way, fearing they would be beaten, both literally and figuratively.

The preacher talked about Daniel in the lions' den and Clarence listened for an answer but found none. The lions ignored Daniel.

He didn't know how long Venitia was going to avoid him in anger but at Sunday dinner she turned to him for answers. "What am I gon' do?" she asked. "They say I browned the team 'cause I play better than the others. They say I stewed the school 'cause I'm there. Like I'm some kinda disease. I don' want to go to school no more. I don' want to play on they team."

"Is school that bad?"

"The teachers are fair. The kids — some of 'em are nice, too nice, like I they simple-minded cousin. Others won't look at me, like they embarrassed or afraid. Mos' don' know what to say to me, like I the family freak. The girls on the team — I broke up they crush; it be the same with any new girl. They jealous, and sometimes round-eyed like they can't believe what I just done, like I'm the ugly sister who married the prince. It just some of the boys showing off, defending petticoats and Ol' Marse Bob like I was General Sherman going to destroy everything in my path."

"I know it's not easy, but I fought for your right to go to that school."

"I done heard all that," she said, not in anger but resignation. "I'm tired of it and yo' do-nothing dreams. The only one proud of yo' being a buffalo soldier is yo'. How come no one ask yo' to join the American Legion, the V.F.W. and them other clubs folks so proud of? They needed yo' and Grampa to die in they place. That's all y'all counted for."

"Lots of folks suffered so you'd have the chance that they never had. We have to believe that all that suffering means something and that our suffering means something too. And that if you can do it, others can do it."

"Yo' ought to been a preacher," she said. "What makes yo' such a patriot? Yo' and all them others that fought for a country that don't even want y'all?"

Her question startled him. He had sung "God Bless America" as loudly and meaningfully as any white boy. He was as proud of what his father had done as any hero's son anywhere. Why did he love a country that had enslaved his people? Where successive waves of newcomers seeking economic opportunity were favored over those who had broken their backs and given their lives for the country? Where waking up every morning meant working harder than anyone else to prove to loafers that you weren't lazy. Where social success required that you take insults to prove to fools your sense of humor.

Why did he love such a country? Maybe because it had cost him so much. Those the country favored with tax breaks, good streets, police protection, quality education didn't die in Korea and Vietnam. Their country had taught them to look out for themselves, to profit from the weakness of others, to take what they could and to give only to gain favor. His country had taught him, and those who fought beside him, that the good of all was more important than what was best for him.

"I guess I'm a patriot because other people suffered to give me what I have. It's not equal and it's not right but I couldn't be what I am if some others hadn't taken a stand, taken an insult, taken a beating. I can think of all those people lynched, their homes burned, their churches bombed, and I can curse the folks who did it and still believe that all white folks aren't like that because some white folks were lynched and their houses burned for trying to help us. I can see a little bit of progress and I can thank God for all those folks, black and white, who tried to make a difference. And I can stand with them and sing, 'God Bless America,' or 'This Land Is My Land,' or 'We Shall Overcome' and that makes me a patriot."

"Yo' can preach 'til yo' blue in the face, don't none of it make sense to me."

"You stay in school and I'll take care of the boys."

"What yo' gon' do?"

She knew he was trained in violence and she feared he would resort to it, but he couldn't answer because he didn't know what he was going to do.

The next morning she dressed, ate breakfast and walked to the bus stop but he could sense her fear. Or maybe she sensed his fear and reflected it. He waited until the bus stopped for her, then went to the barn and worked on the truck, trying to draw comfort from the history on the walls and the bits of machinery that might yet be salvaged.

When time came for the bus to return he was no nearer an answer than before. He walked to the road to be certain the bus stopped. He would walk to the bus stop every day if he had to, and if the bus rolled past him he would follow it until he caught it.

The bus came to a stop, the door precisely before him. When it opened he saw Pie with two friends sitting behind him, smug from their position inside the bus. "We been looking after your little girl," Pie said.

Maybe it was the way he said it, maybe it was the way he tried to smile but couldn't. Clarence held up a hand to stop Venitia, who had started down the steps, and then he climbed into the bus.

"You can't ride this bus," Pie said.

"You can't throw me off," Clarence said before he could stop himself. He wished they would try but they didn't know what to do with him. As he climbed into the bus Venitia watched him, backing to an empty seat and sitting down. He sat beside her.

Venitia's fingers were digging into his arm but he did not turn to her. Pie watched him through the mirror and his friends leaned forward, devising a plan. Clarence wished he had one. Pie closed the door and the bus rolled away.

"What yo' gon' do?" Venitia asked in alarm.

The bus stopped twice more and the students ducked off the bus quickly, not looking back, repudiating them and anything that happened to them.

Clarence thought of taking over the bus, making the boys walk home, parking the bus in front of the superintendent's house and making him explain — he would be arrested, of course, but he would tell the court — there wouldn't be a court, just a crowd of cars around his —

Venitia's nails dug into his arm. They weren't going to the school; they were going to Pie's house.

"They gon' kill us," Venitia said, more in resignation than in fear.

A white man's property was his domain. Black people did not trespass on white property. Clarence knew he was over his head, had been from the beginning, and that he had dragged his daughter into it.

Pie drove the bus to his home, across the yard, close to the front door. The three boys jumped off the bus, almost before it stopped. "Pa," Pie squalled. "Pa. This niggah won't get off the bus."

Royce came out of the house, amazed to see black people in his front yard. Clarence pushed Venitia back on the bus. "Stay there," he cautioned her.

"You done gone too far now, niggah," Pie said. "You gonna git your butt kicked all the way back to Detroit."

In his anger Clarence had blundered into enemy territory unarmed. It was not a new situation for black people and Clarence wondered what others had done in the face of prejudice, violence. They had kept their dignity before those who would deny it. They couldn't make him less than he was. To kill him would be to make him more.

"What are you doing on my place?" Royce asked. It was a warning rather than a question.

"He's not even supposed to be on the bus," Pie said.

"I wanted to know why your boy didn't let my girl off the bus, took her back to school and made her walk home."

Royce looked at Pie in confusion. "What happened, son?"

"Nobody likes her," Pie said. "Nobody wants to have to sit in the bus with her."

"The superintendent said she could go to school, ride the bus. Thought if the superintendent hired your boy to drive the bus he told him to let my girl off at her stop."

"Why didn't you let her off the bus?" Royce asked Pie.

"She took Jill's place on the volleyball team," the boy blurted. "Nobody likes her. It was just a joke."

"She shouldn't a been on that bus in the first place," Royce said. "Why can't you go to your own school? Ride your own bus?"

"There isn't a school for blacks," Clarence said. "The superintendent said she could ride the bus. I thought as a neighbor I should talk to you about it before I talk to the superintendent."

"My boy will do his job. I'll guarantee that. If he has to let her on the bus he'll let her on and he'll let her off at the right place. We have always been law-abiding people." Royce glared at Clarence a moment, then looked away. "I appreciate you coming to me, but you ain't my neighbor. Now get off my place."

"I have a place just down the road. Not long ago you wanted to buy it."

"I still do. I'll make you the same offer I was going to make Jeff."

"You came to me when your well pump broke. Seems to me that makes us neighbors. You offered me the same price you offered Jeff. Seems to me that makes us equal."

"We ain't equal. And even if we were, we ain't the same."

"Jeff wanted me to have what he had, and that's what I intend to have."

"Me too," said Venitia, who had gotten off the bus.

"Jeff was a fool, but I reckon he could do what he wanted to with his place. It was his."

"It's my place now, and I aim to be buried there, and Venitia and her kids and grandkids will be buried beside me. My folks and your folks are going to live side by side for a long time. Maybe we can show them how to get along."

Royce turned and surveyed his place. "What has happened to America that my boy can't choose who he wants to go to school with? Sit with in church? Eat with? I got nothing against you and your kind as long as you leave me and mine alone."

"I've eaten with white folks, slept beside them in foxholes and bunkers. If I'd left them alone there are a few who wouldn't be alive today. When times are bad we fight together. Seems like when times are good we could live together," Clarence said.

"What did you come here for?"

"I wanted to see this boy's father and mother. I wanted to know how they felt about their boy taking a man's job and then not letting a girl off at her bus stop. Then I'm going to tell your son that my daughter will walk home every day if she has to. But the next day she'll play ball as good as she can, even if that's better than some white girl. Nothing is going to make her less than her best."

"She won't have to walk again. Isn't that right, Pie?" Royce asked. "My boy will do what's right."

"Why does she have to be on the team?" Pie asked.

"She's on the team because she's eligible, just like the other girls," Clarence said. "Because the team needs her. Because the coach thinks she's the best player he has."

"Because I want to be on the team," Venitia said.

"If my son gets paid to do a man's job, then I expect him to do a man's work," Royce said. He looked at Pie. "We give fair measure for what we get. We always have; we always will."

"It doesn't matter," Venitia said. "It just makes me stronger."

"We're good people," Royce said. "We don't intend harm to anyone. I don't agree with it, but as long as the law says she can ride the bus, she won't have to walk if my son is driving it. I guarantee that."

"Have you got an outhouse?" Venitia asked.

Harmon's face turned cold. "You can go behind the barn yonder if you have to."

"Oh, I don't have to go," Venitia said. "I just wanted to know how far behind you are." She smiled at her father, turned and started toward home.

"Where are you going?" Royce asked.

"We're walking home," Clarence said. "This is a freedom march, from your place to my place. My girl and I are going to walk home in pride. And tomorrow, she's going to be the best player in school."

"Get back on the bus," Harmon said. "Pie will take you home."

Clarence caught up with Venitia, who looked up at him. She was proud of being black. She was proud of him. She took his hand and as they marched, she sang.

"We're good people," Harmon called after them. "We don't intend to harm nobody."

"You can sit in the front if that's what bothers you," Pie grumbled.

Clarence and Venitia continued their freedom march. They'd have to run to catch up.

How I Won the War

The whole world was at war and everyone had to sacrifice. That's what the movie stars, and even President Roosevelt, said. Dad was in the Pacific. Mother ran the service station and came home dirty every night and so tired she had to rest before fixing supper. "Everyone has to help if we're going to win the war," she said. I walked home after school; we lived on forty acres outside of town. I fed the chickens, hogs and the milk cow, tended the victory garden, swept the floors and washed the dishes. Mother gave me fifty cents a week and I saved the money for a Victory Bond to buy bullets to help Dad fight the war.

Every Friday the teachers sold stamps that you could glue in a little book until you had enough for a Victory Bond. Mother gave me money for a stamp every week in addition to my allowance. Billy Crutchfield bragged that he bought two stamps every week. His dad was the banker, and the government wouldn't let him fight in the war because women couldn't run the bank, Billy said. Harold Tedford bragged about the scrap metal he collected from his dad's farms. He sold it and used the money to go to the picture show every Friday night with Billy Crutchfield and some of the other kids.

Mother said I could use my allowance to go to the picture show if I wanted to, and I did sometimes if it was something special like *Wake Island,* but mostly I saved the money to buy a bond. I was going to save my allowance until I had enough, and when the teacher asked who wanted to buy a stamp I was going to say, "I want to buy a bond." I could imagine the look on Billy's face. Harold's too, and a lot of the other kids.

Harold's brother was a mechanic at an airfield in Kansas and sent Harold wings made of some metal alloy. Harold wore them like his brother was a pilot. Billy's dad was given a collar pin like soldiers wore for leading a bond drive at the bank and Billy wore it to school sometimes. Dad didn't send me any souvenirs; he didn't even write many letters. Mother said there weren't any stores in the Pacific, but I knew it was because he was too busy fighting. I wanted my dad home more than anything and I had saved fifteen dollars when a man came down the road leading a horse.

Not many people came by on horseback anymore, just farmers and ranchers trying to save gas and tires.

I saw them when the horse fell. The man kicked and beat the horse until it got up. He rode a little ways and the horse fell again. The third time it fell, he beat and kicked the horse until it got back on its feet, but it almost fell again when he tried to get back in the saddle. After that the man led the horse until it fell in front of the house. He yelled at the horse, pulled on the reins and kicked it. The horse got halfway to its feet then fell.

I walked out to the road. The man was small and dried up and maybe too old to be in the army. His clothes were dirty and he had an old blanket tied to his saddle. "What's the matter with your horse?" I asked. Its sides were heaving, its neck was lathered and it was blowing bloody foam out of its nostrils.

"Just lazy. You folks couldn't give me a ride into town could you?"

"Nobody here but me," I said.

The man nodded. He studied the horse. "I ain't never going to get to town like this. Sorry sack of . . . bones." He kicked the horse again.

"Is he your horse?" I asked, surprised that anyone would kick his own horse.

"He is until I can sell him for dog food. If I can get him to town." He gave me a sidelong glance. "You don't think your folks might want to buy a horse, do you?"

I wanted a horse more than anything except winning the war and seeing Dad again. "Would you be willing to sell him to me?"

He studied me, not directly but looking at me sideways from under his hat that was torn and too big for his head. "How much you got to buy him with?"

"I got fifteen dollars but I'm saving that to buy a Vict — "

"You just bought yourself a horse."

I was stunned, not just that he accepted but by the speed of it. Nobody bought anything without dickering for a while.

"You ain't going to go back on your word, are you?" he asked.

Dad thought that going back on your word was about the lowest thing a man could do, except maybe being a slacker or hoarding things that were rationed. I wasn't sure how he felt about someone saving money to buy a bond to win the war and then buying a horse for himself with it. "I've been saving to buy a Victory Bond," I said.

"You can't buy no bond for fifteen dollars. Now, if you had a horse, rested him a few days, you could sell him for enough to buy a bond, maybe two bonds."

"Really?" I kneeled in the road and stroked the horse. Its muzzle was hot. Its eyes bulged. "What's his name?"

"This horse? Why, this is . . . Blaze. See that white on his forehead. That's called a blaze. That's how he got his name."

"How you doing, Blaze?" I asked, rubbing behind his ears. The horse eyed me indifferently. For fifteen dollars I could buy a real horse, a horse of my own. Wouldn't Mother be surprised? She might be disappointed that I didn't buy a bond, but when I explained that I could sell Blaze for two bonds — Blaze nudged me and I hugged his lathered neck. I knew I couldn't sell Blaze, not even for two bonds.

"I wouldn't sell him except that, well, in Fort Worth they make airplanes to fight the war. I want to help make them planes and I can't take the horse with me. That's why I'm willing to let you have him for fifteen dollars. That is some bargain, boy. Patriotic too."

I thought of me and Blaze riding up in the schoolyard and all the kids watching. Then I thought of Dad in the Pacific. "I don't know," I said.

"Get back and I'll get the son of a . . . I'll get him up so you can look at him," the man said, ready to kick Blaze some more.

"No. Don't."

"I want you to see the kind of horse you're getting."

"He's fine. I just planned to buy a Victory Bond."

"Well, I got to get him up and get on the road then. I don't want to hold up them airplanes just because he's tired."

I didn't want to hold up the war effort either; I just couldn't make up my mind to let my dream come true when everybody else was sacrificing to win the war.

"You know anything about horses, son?"

"No, sir," I admitted, although I feared he was going to tell me I didn't know enough to buy a horse.

"This here is a thoroughbred, the finest horse in the world."

I could buy Blaze for fifteen dollars, let him rest for a couple of days and give him to the army, and maybe after the war was over and Dad and Blaze came home, they'd give him back. After they didn't need him anymore. I thought of Blaze leading a charge, or maybe dragging a cannon up at just the right time.

"Can a thoroughbred pull a heavy load?"

"You let old Blaze rest a couple of days and he can pull any wagon you got."

I didn't have a wagon but Harold Tedford's father did. Maybe he would loan me the wagon and I could hitch Blaze to it and pick up scrap metal. And I'd use that money to buy a bond. I could take the horse to school and during recess give kids a ride for a nickel, and when the teacher asked who wanted to buy a stamp, I'd pour the money out on her desk and tell her I wanted as many as I could buy. For a moment I saw President Roosevelt appearing at a school assembly and calling me and Blaze up on the stage to thank us for the bonds we had bought. Or the army might give me a collar pin like they gave Billy's dad.

"Get back, kid. I got to get the horse up and get going."

"Wait," I said. "I'll get the money." I ran to the house and when I got back he was kicking Blaze again. "What are you doing?"

"I didn't sell the saddle and bridle," he said. He had already pulled off the bridle and he hit Blaze with the reins.

I said, "Don't hit him anymore. I'll help you get the saddle."

We tugged and pulled and he kicked at the horse until we got the saddle. With the bridle in his hand, he started down the road dragging the saddle. I sat beside Blaze and put my arms around his lathered neck. "He won't hurt you anymore," I said, as glad as Blaze was that the man had gone. "You rest a while and when you feel better I'll put you in the lot."

Blaze avoided looking me in the eye. I went to the barn, got a tub and started pulling grass for the horse. While I pulled grass, I thought of how we'd look riding to school.

"He's a thoroughbred," I'd say. "Finest horse in the world." I'd give kids rides when they bought Victory stamps, and I'd collect scrap metal, and if they needed me to I could ride Blaze around town looking for spies and saboteurs.

I heard a car honking, saw a cloud of dust coming down the road and remembered Blaze lying in the middle of it. I ran to the road waving and yelling, "Stop." The car skidded into the bar ditch. "Get that horse out of the road before someone runs over it," the driver yelled. He stopped to pick up the man with the saddle, and I knew then that he would get to Fort Worth and that I had done the right thing to buy Blaze.

I also knew I was going to have to get Blaze out of the road. I caught hold of his mane but I couldn't move him. I got a rope from the barn and put it around his neck, but I still couldn't budge Blaze. I got the tub of grass and tried to coax him but Blaze ignored it. I sat down in the road, ready to cry. "You're going to get run over," I said. "Then I can't ride you or collect scrap or anything."

I went to the barn, filled a bucket with water and carried it to him. Blaze stuck his nose in the bucket and turned it over. I filled it again but he wouldn't drink it. I dipped water out of the bucket and washed the blood off his muzzle. I went to the house, got the slip off my pillow, and sat down beside Blaze, ready to wave down any car that came down the road. The first car was Mother.

"Jimmy, what are you doing in the road?"

"I can't get Blaze to move," I said. "Someone is going to run over him."

"Whose horse is it?"

"He's mine," I said, afraid my mother would think buying a horse instead of a bond wasn't the right thing to do. My chin was trembling and I couldn't make it stop. "I bought him with the money I was saving to buy a bond and now I can't get him out of the road and he's going to get run over."

Mother parked the car in front of the house and walked

back to the road. She sat down and put her arm around me. She smelled like gasoline. "Tell me what happened," she said.

Between sniffs and nose wipes I told her about Blaze falling because he was tired, and the man beating him, and buying Blaze to buy bonds, and the car coming and Blaze not eating, and now I didn't know what to do.

"He was a bad man. He sold you an old horse that is dying."

"No. He's a thoroughbred, the finest kind of horse. He's just tired." I ducked my head so she wouldn't see any tears.

She hugged me closer and kissed the top of my head the way she did sometimes. "See all that gray on his face," she said. "He's an old horse and he's been mistreated and overworked. I don't think he's going to live." I knew she didn't think Blaze was a thoroughbred either. "You go in the house. I'll go get Mr. Tedford."

"Will he make Blaze feel better?"

"I think he'll want to put him out of his misery. We don't want him to suffer anymore, do we?" She put her hand on Blaze's head.

"Could we get the horse doctor? To be sure he's not just tired."

"He could be anywhere in the county, and with gas rationing —" Her voice trailed off. "I guess we ought to give your horse a chance."

"He said when Blaze got rested he would be worth two bonds. If he can get well I can sell rides on him. I can use him to collect scrap. I'll use the money to buy bonds."

"I'll get the vet but don't get your hopes up about the horse getting better. Go on to the house now. Don't you have some chores?"

"Can I stay out here with him? So a car doesn't hit him?"

She sighed. "Okay. Go get the lantern and light it. I don't want you out here in the road after dark without a lantern. As soon as you hear a car you start waving that lantern. But not so fast that you blow the light out. Are you going to be scared here by yourself?"

"No, ma'am." It wasn't exactly a lie. I wouldn't be scared if Blaze got up so I could ride him away if something bad came along.

I sat close beside Blaze so I could touch him. I had always wanted a horse, and now I had one even if he was old and tired. It was a long time before Mother came back with the vet, and only one car came along. The driver said, "I hope your horse gets to feeling better." He knew it was my horse and he knew Blaze and I were doing the best we could.

I thought about the war, and if I was being a slacker because I gave my Victory Bond for a horse. I thought about Dad and how I would have to explain what I had done.

Blaze's head started nodding, like he was trying to go to sleep. Then he put his head down and stretched out his legs like he was pawing. Then he just stopped. I knew he was dead before the vet got there, but I didn't tell Mom or the vet. I just couldn't. The vet said I had done all I could for him and that he would send somebody out to get him. "Not too late," Mom said. He looked at me and nodded. I knew Mom wanted them to take Blaze away while I was in school.

Mom and I sat with Blaze for a while. Just sitting there, not saying anything. Then I said, "For a little while my dream came true."

"Even in wartime, a lot of dreams come true for a little while."

"You don't think I let Dad down?"

"I think your father would have done the same thing."

"Really?"

"It takes more than just bullets to win a war," she said.

I didn't tell the kids at school about Blaze because I was afraid they'd laugh at me. But when I told Dad, he said Mother was right.

A Boy and His Dog

The jeep dropped Iowa and the dog beside the wide, sluggish river. Straw-roofed hootches were scattered between the road and the river, tucked into folds, ravines, under areca and palm trees. Near the center of the ville was a marketplace, an open square of masonry buildings that had been scarred by bullets and shrapnel. Iowa stared at the Vietnamese who watched the dog from their hootches. To them the dog was not a savior but a meal.

Iowa slung his rifle and led the dog down the footpath to the market. A squad of Marines was scattered among the scarred buildings. They ignored Iowa and the dog. He was a Marine, but he wasn't one of them and they didn't want to know him if he was going to get blown away the first day.

Iowa studied the Marines, who seemed at home in the

ville although they were alert, their eyes wary. He had walked into unfamiliar units before and he had learned to recognize who was in charge. Command hung heavy on young shoulders. He spotted the long, thin, pinched face that showed the strain of leading the squad and protecting the villagers. A corporal, Iowa guessed, short of his own twenty years and three stripes. The kind of kid who a year ago hung around garages looking for a job and lounged around pool halls looking for a friend.

Iowa led the lean, hungry-looking German Shepherd to him. "I'm Iowa," he said. He wasn't from Iowa, but his name was Davenport and when he said "Davenport," someone always said, "Iowa." "This is Fat Chance," he said. "Don't worry if he bites you, he's had all his shots."

The corporal was not amused; they never were. By the time he was called in they had already lost some of their buddies to mines and booby traps. Mines did that to a man — robbed him of his sense of humor, made him thoughtful of his limbs and the soft flesh below the flak jacket.

The corporal stared at him, hands on hips, thin shoulders set as though still wearing a pack. "Been in the bush before?" he asked.

There it was. His uniform was clean and so was his face, so they thought he had a slide. It was true that after three days in the field he took the dog to Da Nang for ten days of retraining, but for those three days he was walking point. "Yeah," he said. If the corporal wanted to know about the Purple Heart, let him ask.

"This area is a bear and a half," the corporal said.

If it wasn't bad they wouldn't have needed him. Iowa squeezed the loose skin on the dog's back. Fat Chance looked up at him with a grin.

"Three years ago Charlie blew this place away. Threw grenades in the bunkers and burned the hootches," the corporal explained. The Americans rebuilt the ville, but the

Vietnamese wouldn't live in it unless the Americans protected them. The Americans sent a squad of fourteen Marines and a Navy corpsman as a token of their pledge. "We've been able to keep Charlie out of the ville, but we got to be able to patrol the area. That's why we need the dog. I hope he's up to it," the corporal said, walking away.

"He knows what to do," Iowa said. Fat Chance had been trained for eighteen weeks in the States and six weeks in Okinawa, at a cost of sixteen thousand dollars, and every time Iowa went into the bush, he bet his life on the dog. If he got back to the world in one piece it would be because of Fatty.

"I'm not leaving you, Fat Chance," he said. The dog studied his face. When the dog handlers went home, the dogs were turned over to ARVN units, but the ARVN didn't know how to use the dogs, so they ate them. He had heard that. "When I go, you go with me. I'll buy you if I have to." He had heard he could do that, and he was going to. Even if he had to pay for the dog's training. He would borrow the sixteen thousand dollars. He and the dog had been through too much together. Fat Chance rubbed his head against Iowa's arm. Iowa scratched the dog's ears.

When they had given him the dog, they told him the dog would become closer to him than anything he had ever known, closer than his mother, closer than his girlfriend. "Fat chance," he had said. But it was true. Fat Chance was the only thing he believed in anymore, the only thing that was real.

Another of the men approached. He was a big, dark Chicano with sad eyes and a mustache that slanted downwards. Iowa recognized him too — the corpsman with his litany of questions. "Name? Blood type? Zap number? Carry your battle dressings in your right trouser pocket so I'll know where to find them. I don't want to have to use mine."

Iowa led Fat Chance through the Marines and into an empty hootch where it was cooler. The heat kicked the dog's ass. He poured water in a canteen cup and watched Fat Chance gratefully lap it up. Iowa carried twenty-two canteens of water when he was in the field. Four of them were for himself.

He sat down beside Fat Chance and groomed the dog, then worked him before feeding him. Sit, lie, stand, come, stay, using first voice, then hand signals. He had to keep the dog hungry. Fat Chance worked for food. And to please his master.

Iowa felt the dog go tense, alert, before he saw the children squatting in the entrance to the hootch, their eyes and mouths wide. The trained dog was the closest thing to a circus they had ever seen. "Di-di," he yelled at the children, waving them away. "Di-di." He turned to the dog. "Sit." The dog did not seem to hear. When he gave the command again, Fat Chance looked at him before obeying, then turned to stare out the doorway.

"Fatty," he said sharply to get the dog's attention. "Old Fatty doesn't like being in the ville." He knew how the dog felt. There were too many things lying around and any of them could be booby trapped. "Lighten up," he said, trying to relax himself. They were a team and when Iowa was jittery, Fat Chance was jittery. When Iowa was careless, Fat Chance was careless. "Nothing we can't handle," he said.

Iowa had volunteered as a dog handler because he liked dogs and he had pictured himself and the dog patrolling an airfield. He didn't even know that dogs could detect mines and booby traps. Then they started teaching him about fuzes — pressure fuzes, percussion fuzes, friction fuzes, pressure-release fuzes, tension-release fuzes, electric fuzes — blind, unfeeling things that could maim or kill. No matter how easily or quickly you detected them, it was always a close call. They were aimed at your balls, at your mind. You couldn't defeat a mine; you could only disable it. There was no victory over a mine, only a reprieve. Until the year was up or one of them got you. Whichever came first.

Iowa wanted no part of looking for mines; he wanted no part of the dog.

"You volunteered," they said.

"I didn't know."

"But you volunteered," they said.

He had hated the dog then.

The first mine the dog had found had been a round from a 105 howitzer rigged to be command-detonated. Iowa had been scared but relieved, knowing that if he made a mistake he would not have time to regret it. That had been the first reprieve.

He had gained other reprieves but going into the field got harder each time. He had seen handlers who had gotten lazy, or careless, or tired or frightened, or had let their dog get lazy, careless, tired or frightened. The lucky ones died and few of them died quickly. The others went home to spend the rest of their lives in a wheelchair with someone forking food into what used to be their mouth, and wiping the new ass the doctors gave them. With nothing to remember but the click of that little spring and no one to hate but themselves. Booby. Betrayed by their own hand.

He was an outsider and he would die friendless, alone. The others had buddies, someone they were tight with, someone who cared. When he knelt over one of the implacable killers, feeling for its secret heart with hands as gentle and persuasive as those of a lover, he needed to know that someone was watching, someone cared. And afterwards when his hands trembled, his legs jerked, his eyes twitched, when the fear that he had held at arm's length began slipping home so that he was afraid to relax, afraid to close his eyes, afraid to sleep, he needed someone he could talk to, someone who understood.

He needed someone on those nights when his body remembered, his muscles getting tighter and tighter until he had to get up, had to move. Had to have someone. That's when he and the dog became a team. Fat Chance shared his loneliness, his fear. Fat Chance whined and pawed and tugged until Iowa grabbed him around the neck and, wrestling and growling, together they lost the fear in play. They faced the trail together side by side and if they died they would die together. Iowa and Fat Chance were tight.

Until Fat Chance had found the booby trap. It was a homemade device — the best and worst kind. Best because they were crudely made and many were duds. Worst because their crudity made them eccentric. They did not always respond cause and effect, tension and release, striker and percussion, detonator and charge, like well-made machines. Sometimes they blew themselves up. Sometimes they killed the man who set them. Iowa had seen that once — a family, mother, father and three children, who looked as though they had been squatting around the mine while the father planted it. Their faces were frozen in surprise, their mouths and eyes gaping.

This machine consisted of nails in a C-ration can with a fuze from a Chicom grenade. Iowa was defuzing it when he heard the spring click. The fuze's delay gave him time to jerk his hands clear and to cover the grenade with a flak jacket. Luckily the charge was weak and the flak jacket took most of the nails, but one hit him in the leg and Fat Chance was hit in the neck.

After that, Iowa could not sleep. When his breath clicked in his nose he awoke in a sweat, heart pounding in his chest. When the sheet brushed against his leg he was afraid to move, convinced he had touched a trip wire. He couldn't go to the piss tube without walking in someone else's tracks. He jumped out of a moving jeep in Da Nang because he saw a hubcab that looked like a mine lying in the road. He stood frozen in the Freedom Hill PX afraid to pick up a carton of cigarettes, convinced there was a pressure-release mine beneath the stack. A pogue had grabbed two cartons, and Iowa had dropped to the floor and covered his head.

That had brought him to the attention of the gunnery

sergeant. The gunny was at least thirty, with white streaks in his close-cropped hair and creases in his leathery face. Iowa had never seen him when he didn't have a mine in his hand, his fingers probing its inner parts. The gunny had no nails on his twisted fingers and scars ran up his arms, his neck and the side of his face. "We're going to retrain you and the dog," the gunny said. "You have to get your confidence back, and you have to regain the confidence of the dog. You failed him. You caused him pain. He'll forgive you but you'll have to earn his trust."

At dusk the corporal said, "We're moving." Iowa found his place near the end of the column. They walked through the deserted marketplace, splashed through puddles of water, followed a cart-wide street that had been churned into a quagmire, then a footpath, slipping and skidding between the darkened hootches. It wasn't good for the dog; it confused him. Although there were no lights in the hootches, Fat Chance could hear the Vietnamese whispering and moving around inside.

Fat Chance stopped abruptly, ears up, nose pointing at something in the darkness. Iowa knew there were no mines in the ville, but he had to check it out to avoid embarrassing the dog. He got down on his hands and knees in the mud and dug up some discarded communication wire.

"What are you doing?" the corporal asked, hands on hips, angry that the squad had stopped. His words hissed as he tried to keep his voice down. "There aren't any mines in the ville. Now keep up."

Iowa picked up Fat Chance and carried him over his shoulder to keep him from alerting at suspicious wire or disturbed earth and from being confused when Iowa ignored the signal. Iowa knew the others were ridiculing him for carrying the dog, and he was furious. They had no respect for Fat Chance. The dog knew what was going on, and if they didn't respect him, he wouldn't work for them.

The squad passed through a group of Vietnamese PFs who guarded a trail into the ville. The men of the ville — the PFs — had been given rifles to protect their families, but they were untrained and untrusted. The Marines walked down the trail to a cemetery. Some of the Marines took up ambush positions among the circular graves and the rest took a different trail back to the ville and faded into the hootches. The corporal pointed Iowa into a thatch-roofed, bamboo-sided hootch with a single doorway opening to the outside. An inner bamboo wall divided the hootch into two rooms. Iowa knew a Vietnamese family was on the other side of the wall by the way Fat Chance acted.

Iowa sat down on the dirt floor and wiped the dog's feet on his jacket. He was trying to calm the dog when a Vietnamese child stuck her head around the partition, and before Iowa saw her, Fat Chance lunged over his shoulder with a snarl and sank his teeth into the girl's face. The girl screamed, Iowa yelled "Down," and the corporal was in the hootch.

"Get the dog outside," he hissed, "and send the doc."

Iowa sat on the muddy ground outside the hootch, cradling the dog in his arms, trying to distract him from the girl, but Fat Chance looked at the hootch and quivered, growling low in his throat. The corporal and corpsman came outside. "Tore up her face," Doc said, looking not at the corporal but at Iowa. "Her eye is okay and I can sew up her lip, but she'll have a hole in her cheek unless we can get her to Da Nang."

"They won't send a medevac out here at night," the corporal said. "And if they did, Charlie would start dropping mortars on this place and we'd get a lot more people hurt." Doc shrugged, his eyes and mustache drooping. "Do what you can and I'll call the lieutenant."

The corpsman went back into the hootch and the corporal went to look for the radioman. When he returned Iowa knew the lieutenant had refused a medevac. "That little girl is going to have a hole in her cheek for the rest of her life," the corporal said. "Our first civilian casualty in three weeks. I hope that dog is worth it."

Iowa sat outside in the mud, unwilling to take the dog into another hootch. When the doc came out he stopped and looked at Iowa and Fat Chance in disgust. Iowa ignored him. If he got torn up by a mine, the corpsman would have to try to save his life, his legs, whether he liked him or not. And as long as Iowa was alive, he'd see that Fat Chance got medical treatment like any other Marine.

He could hear the little girl's muffled sobs, and he remembered the pain and fright in her eyes, but it wasn't Fat Chance's fault. They should keep the dog at the CP, away from the Vietnamese, until they were on the trail. The Vietnamese made him nervous. But when the squad got on the trail, they were going to be glad to have Fat Chance. "We'll show them," he said. Fat Chance looked at him and grinned.

The squad moved twice more during the night, slipping silently through the ville and sliding into hootches. At first light they walked through a mist to the edge of the ville where they waited. When it was light enough to see the trail, Iowa and Fat Chance took the point. They hadn't gone five hundred meters before the dog found a mine.

"Sure glad you're in front of me," said the second man in the column. Even among the young he looked conspicuously young. He had tried to grow a mustache but had barely grown a nose. His tousled blond hair still defied his mother's efforts to tame it.

"You take care of the snipers and we'll take care of the mines," Iowa said.

"Say it," Blondie said. Iowa saw that the men were more relaxed now, watching the terrain instead of their feet.

Iowa carried the dog across a sluggish stream. On the other side was an uncultivated area of low weeds bordered by tree lines. Fat Chance discovered a metal tube buried in the ground. The column stopped while Iowa dug around it. He found nothing but told Blondie to pass the word to avoid it. Blondie nodded, appreciation in his look. Fat Chance had their attention now.

The trail led them through the tree line and beside a swift river. It was not a good place. There was too much to see. Iowa was busy watching not only for mines and trip wires but also ambushes and snipers. He knew the others were watching, but he was the first man on the trail. The dog alerted at a burned-out flare hanging by its parachute from a low bush. "Good boy, Fatty," Iowa said, praising and patting the dog. Fat Chance licked his face.

The trail turned from the river and became a low, narrow tunnel through a grove of trees. Iowa was doubled over when the dog's tail brushed a limb and a round from a 60mm mortar fell at his feet. Iowa was unable to move, to take his eyes off the hard green and yellow cylinder.

"It's a dud," he heard Blondie saying in awe. He didn't believe it. Even when he saw that the safety wire was still in place he did not believe it. Without taking his eyes off the round, Iowa dropped slowly to his knees as though it were an object of veneration. Mouth open, tongue extended, he gingerly picked up the shell and moved it off the trail.

He sat back on his heels and took a deep breath. The dog had made a mistake. Iowa was alive because some man had made a bigger one. Iowa sat down on the trail and put his arms around the dog, looking in his eyes to see if Fat Chance knew he had made a mistake. Fat Chance looked ashamed.

"What's the holdup?" the corporal asked.

"The dog is tired," Iowa said. "A dog can only work about forty-five minutes and then his attention starts wandering and he has to be rested."

"We got to keep moving or Charlie will hit us while we're stopped."

Iowa gave Fat Chance some water and when the dog lay down, Iowa snapped his lead and urged him down the trail. Blondie was not so close now and Iowa could feel himself beginning to hunch a little. Something was missing, some link between him and the dog was gone. Iowa straightened. "Me and Fat Chance are tight," he said softly. "Good old Fatty. We're a team." The dog did not look up at him but he ducked his head a little. "When Fat Chance is tired, Iowa has to be twice as alert."

Half an hour later there was a shuddering blast of noise and heat as Blondie disappeared in a cloud of smoke, dirt and steel.

"Freeze," the corporal screamed. "Freeze." The men were caught in childhood postures, somewhere between standing and their impulse to bury their faces in the ground. Smoke and dust hung in the air, but Iowa could see the crumpled body. He forced his eyes away, forced them to search for other mines. He tried to untangle the dog from his feet without moving them.

"Doc up, Doc up," the corporal yelled. "Keep your eyes open. They'll hit us while we're not moving."

The corpsman made his way up the column, causing a little flurry of concern when he came close to another man, trying to step in footsteps that had proven safe, past a steel helmet that hung from a bush, a flak jacket on the trail, to the wounded man who lay in a tangled green, white and red heap. "You're going to be okay," the corpsman said. "We're going to get you out of here. You're going to be okay."

"Is it bad?" Blondie asked. "It don't hardly hurt. I can stand it."

Iowa crouched, holding the excited dog, trying not to see, not to hear, not to smell. He had made a mistake. He and Fat Chance had made a mistake. He could feel the hatred of the others. Their buddy had gotten hurt because of him.

"Jesus, it's not as bad as I thought it would be," Blondie said, and tried to cough. Even now his screwed-up face resembled a baby about to cry more than a man in pain. "I knew it would hurt, but it's not so bad."

"You got the best corpsman in the world," Doc said quietly. "You just hang on. Keep breathing now. Open them eyes. We're going to get you out of here. You're almost home. Just hang on a little bit."

There were other sounds. The radioman calling for a medevac, muttered curses, mumbled prayers, the whimpering of the dog. Iowa was too close. He could smell torn entrails, hot blood, fresh excrement. He could feel the dog trembling. Something welled up inside of him and he tried to spit.

"What's that?" the wounded man screamed, his blond head jerking from the ground, catching sight of his intestines fouled with dirt and bits of leaves. "Oh God, oh God, help me. God. Noooo."

"You're not going to die," Doc said, putting himself between the man and his wounds. "Look at me. Come on, man, look at me. Don't close them eyes. Look at me. It's just dirt, man. We'll get that off. A little dirt, man, that don't mean nothing. Look at me," he said, giving Blondie a shake. "Get a grip, you bastard. Open them eyes. Breathe; don't die. Just a little while. It's just dirt; lots of guys look worse. Breathe, you son of a bitch. Open them eyes. Breathe, you bastard. You — " The corpsman slumped a little, wiped his wet hands on the clean part of Blondie's uniform and turned to look at the others. "He quit. I could have saved him. He just quit."

"You did what you could," the corporal said.

Eyes darting, the men stood in their mock statue poses as though only the space they occupied was safe. The corporal was the first to straighten. "Change the medevac from emergency to permanent routine," he ordered the radioman. "We'll carry him until we find a sit-down for the chopper. Okay, let's move."

Iowa looked up in amazement. He couldn't believe it. He couldn't believe they were going to get back on the trail. "Fat Chance is tired," he said, trying to explain the distracted dog who cowered at his feet. "He has to be rested."

"You killed that man," the corporal yelled, his scream almost a cry. "You killed him. Now get that dog on the trail."

"I ain't walking point," Iowa said. "This is suicide."

"You got the point. Had you rather walk it with or without the dog?"

Iowa looked at the corporal. He didn't believe it. "It's up to you," the corporal said. "Sergeant." The corporal was squad leader, but Iowa was the ranking man, expected to demonstrate leadership. Iowa looked at the others, looking for some hint of reason, of mercy. No one looked at him, no one said anything. He was an outsider. They didn't want to know him. He had no one. No one but Fat Chance.

Iowa looked at the trail ahead of him. It was an evil way, filled with treacherous depressions and dark passages. Vines and creepers waved malignly and sinister shadows slid along the ground. "Ain't no way," he said. "Ain't no way."

"With or without the dog," the corporal said.

Iowa looked at the dog. Fat Chance was asleep at his feet. He thought of shooting the dog. He could say it was anger. He could say it was an accident. He wouldn't have to walk point then. He hit the dog on the head with his open hand. He hit him again and again. Fat Chance whined and ducked, trying to escape the blows. "Wake up, damn it." The others crouched low, expecting an explosion.

"Go," he said. The dog looked around, confused and uncertain. Iowa hit him again and the dog cowered at his feet. "God hates a coward," Iowa said. It was his personal creed. It was all he had left. "Death before dishonor." He took a step, placing his foot carefully on the treacherous ground. The earth seemed to slide away from him. His stomach sank. He could hear little noises bubbling in his throat. He took another step, the dog at his heel.

"Don't crowd him," the corporal yelled. "Keep your interval. And keep your eyes open. He can't do it all."

Sweat rolled down Iowa's face and his knees trembled. His eyes bounced from object to object. He stopped, took a deep breath, wiped his eyes, forced himself to look. Everything was suspicious. Rocks seemed to have been turned over, twigs bent, earth disturbed. He snapped the dog's lead to get his attention.

One step at a time he took through the long afternoon, expecting the earth to erupt beneath him, offering up first his feet, then his legs, then his arms, to keep his manhood.

A helicopter came to pick up Blondie, bringing a brief respite. Iowa watered the dog and let him rest. After the helicopter left, Fat Chance was alert for a while, finding a mine before missing the trip wire to a claymore aimed down the trail. Iowa caught the dog just in time.

Iowa never expected to see the ville again. He led the others to the relative safety inside and kept walking until he reached the river. Fat Chance walked beside him, head down, eyes closed to slits. Iowa dropped to the muddy ground and tried to shake out a cigarette with trembling fingers. Now that he could relax, his arms and legs jerked. Fat Chance sat down beside him and licked his ear. Iowa shoved him away. "You ripped it. We were a team and you ripped it."

He inhaled deeply and exhaled with a sigh, waiting for the tightness in his skull to ease. Fat Chance pawed at his arm. Iowa ignored him.

The corporal sat down beside Iowa and handed him a beer. Iowa held the can to his head. "It wasn't my fault," he said.

"He was our friend," the corporal said.

"It's like a sniper or an ambush," Iowa said. "I can't be responsible for everything that happens. It could have been me that was killed."

"There it is. It was supposed to be you."

"It ain't right," Iowa said. The beer went down his throat like water. "You're supposed to have two dogs, two handlers and rotate them on the point. The dog got tired. It wasn't his fault."

"You think he'll be better tomorrow?" Iowa looked at the corporal, refusing to understand. "The trail we're checking tomorrow is going to be worse."

Iowa tilted the can of beer again and discovered it was empty. He looked at Fat Chance and turned away. "I can't go out with this dog," he said. "I don't trust this dog."

Fat Chance whined and pawed at Iowa, trying to gain his affection, trying to insinuate his head under Iowa's arm. "Fool," Iowa said, backhanding the dog. Fat Chance recoiled and lay whimpering at his feet. "I put my life in his hands. I've never believed in anything the way I believed in that fool."

"This trail is bad," the corporal said. "We got to have a dog."

"I don't have to work with a dog I don't trust. That's a rule. We're a team. We got to trust —" He could see the trail ahead of him, laced with trip wires, festooned with booby traps, paved with mines. His nightmare had come true. His jaws clicked. "I got to go to the rear. I got to get a new dog."

"What happens to this one?"

Iowa shrugged. "A trained dog like this — you can't send him back home."

"I'll have to tell the lieutenant," the corporal said. "So he can get us a better dog." He waited for an answer.

"I can't let the dog down," Iowa said. "After all we been through."

"Hey, man, nobody is deciding for you."

"That's what the war is all about, isn't it? Loyalty. Sticking by your friends. Well, isn't it? Isn't that why we're here?"

"Let me know what to tell the lieutenant," the corporal said. He patted Iowa on the shoulder, got up and walked away.

"I didn't even know they had dogs for mines," Iowa yelled after him.

Fat Chance rubbed his head against Iowa's knee. Iowa pulled the dog into his lap and scratched the soft place behind his ears. Fat Chance pawed, wanting to play. "Me and Fatty," Iowa said, putting his head against the dog's head. "Me and Fatty."

Iowa searched his pockets for food and gave the dog a morsel. "You're the best, Fatty. Best dog in the world. I'd do anything for you. Anything but this." The dog gulped down the food and licked Iowa's face. Iowa gave him another bite. "We can't make it together. Ain't no way." He was feeding the dog steadily now. "It's a long way back to the world, Fatty, and we got our own trails to walk. We're not a team anymore. This is goodbye."

When the dog had eaten all of his food, Iowa opened his C rations. Beef patties in gravy. He took one of the greasy patties in his hand and fed it to the dog. "Atta boy, Fatty. Eat all you want," he said, feeding him another. "You don't have to be hungry anymore."

Fat Chance looked at him and grinned.

Fraternities

It had been a silly argument, as most of their arguments were. Why did she have to work late? When were they going to start a family? Why couldn't they have real friends? It began when his wife announced she had won her company's all-expenses-paid trip to France. For two. It had been a hard fight but she had won their attention and their respect.

Paul hadn't wanted to come to France or any other place where he had to use funny money to buy a beer. He was bored with the others on the tour who rubbed their hands and rolled their eyes over statues and cathedrals so old they were falling apart and rubbed their stomachs and rolled their tongues around meat that hadn't been properly aged.

The weather was damp, the rivers dirty, the streets crowded, the beer warm, the whiskey overpriced, and he disliked the prissy guide who waved his umbrella in the air while insisting that everyone crowd around. "Everyone" meaning he was supposed to get tight with the old hippie with the stringy hair, the May/December lovers — he May, she December — who were always late, the young professor who corrected the guide on every painter, church, street and date and spoke only French to two coeds, the two couples from Dallas who dripped diamonds, Rolexes and Nikons and treated everyone else like FNGs. Paul hoped to never see any of them again.

After several days of riding in a bus, standing in line, staring, gaping, eating, smiling and posing with the group, he had vowed it was the last group tour he would ever take. Then his wife had asked who they should sit with at dinner, the May-December lovers, the hippie fag, the professor who knew no subject on which he could not lecture in two languages or the Dallas couples who made it obvious that the others were olives in their champagne.

Paul had struggled out of pack, platoon and pride and into suit, smile and service, he had exchanged esprit de corps for esprit de commerce, but this was too much. He didn't mind that she made more than he; he wished they'd pay her what she was worth. But why did he have to suck up to people he didn't even like? Why couldn't he and she eat alone? he had sensibly asked. Because it wouldn't look right, she had predictably said.

"To hell with looks," he said. "Look at them. Pogues, every one of them."

He had agreed to come despite his vow that he would never set foot in another foreign country where they ate strange food and spoke a strange language, not even Canada. He had spent all night on an airplane although he had long ago vowed that if he ever got his feet on the ground again he would never go any higher than the second floor. He had carried bags and stood in line although he had vowed never to stand in another line, not even for an automobile license. After breaking these sacred vows for her, he had hoped that she might allow them one evening of fun.

Either Paul had not expressed himself clearly or his wife had failed to understand because they went to dinner with the others. After a few get-acquainted drinks. During which the hippie said he had spent the war in Amsterdam blowing grass, the Dallas men shrugged off the war because it had not only been inconvenient to their careers, it had been dangerously inconvenient, and the college professor, who had been two years old during the Tet offensive, said the United States started the war to prevent multiculturalism at home.

He had said nothing but perhaps had drunk too much. And perhaps he could have been more affable when his wife decided they would intrude themselves at the dinner table of their "friends from Dallas." "To get to know them," she said. Their friends from Dallas had talked about fraternities and sororities at SMU and whatever-happened-to while he attempted to cauterize his steak with alcohol. He had been totally ignored until one of the men asked if he had belonged to Kappa Alpha something. "No," he said. His fraternity was Khe Sahn, although he had also pledged Quang Tri, Cam Lo and Phu Bai.

He had a couple more drinks to celebrate his renewed isolation. It wasn't really Khe Sahn anyway, not the Khe Sahn they knew through the media, the Khe Sahn where men cowered in bunkers and the same wrecked airplane was presented as "new" news every night on television screens. Like most of the Marines, he had been on one of the hills where the fighting took place, the hills that overlooked Khe Sahn that was never attacked, that was really the rear and was the only Khe Sahn most of the hand-wringing reporters knew.

He rose above it all, savored his drinks, muttered witty asides and ignored his wife's glances that were intended to provoke his best behavior.

They had scarcely gotten back to their room when his wife

said he had been rude to "people who could help us." While he was in Vietnam she had fought battles at home, school and work, and her motto was "always network."

He poured himself a drink while suggesting that, a model of tolerance, he had ignored their ignorance. "I didn't say anything," he insisted.

"It's the way you didn't say anything," she said. "And when you did you were insulting."

Paul averred he had been witty with his remarks that cuisine was the French word for raw, that the only people who started at the top were grave diggers and that the three most overrated things in the world were French wines, French gardens and SMU. He had another drink while thinking of additional witty names to call "their important friends" other than Dallas sods, Smu snots and Little D Big Asses.

She cried that she had stood by him while he was in Vietnam — why couldn't he support her in her battle? Having long ago vowed never again to stay where whatever he did wasn't enough, Paul had stalked out of the room and out of the hotel. Hadn't he come on this trip? Hadn't he thanked her bosses for "giving" her the trip when she had clearly earned it? Hadn't he smiled when her supervisor kissed her and wished her "bon voyage and try not to lose soldier-boy over there"?

They always pretended that he was holding her back because he wasn't as educated, as sophisticated as they, but they were the ones holding her back, saying she wasn't "ready," didn't have the "contacts," wasn't in the "right circles."

Too angry to return to the room and renew the battle, too worked up to stand still, he strode down the damp and unfamiliar streets, popping into bars for an occasional drink.

That was how he came to discover himself at a table with a half-finished drink before him. He raised his head to survey his surroundings. The sight was impressive. He was in a dive in some unknown quarter of the city with native cutthroats who appeared insulted by his mere presence. Nodding to them politely, he raised his drink and took a sip to steady his mind. Whiskey. Bad whiskey. Damn foreigners. They were offended that he was drinking American whiskey instead of wine or cognac or something. The bartenders were always suggesting he try the local product. He wondered if he had repeated his witticism that wine was the French attempt to make vinegar.

As he put down his drink he noticed the local assassins were still staring. He had seen that look before. In English it meant get out before we throw you out. No problem. He didn't want to be there anyway. His passion had cooled and he was ready to go back to the hotel; the frigid silence would not keep him awake for long. He would give the bartender a big tip and say "taxi" a few times. Was taxi French or should he say cab? He would try both. Maybe the bartender would call a cab if this place had a telephone. At least point him to a major street where he might find a cab.

He reached in his pants' pocket only to find the pocket empty. No sweat. He had brought credit cards, the universal passport. He reached in his coat pocket for his wallet to find the pocket empty. He had placed his watch, his keys and his wallet on the hotel dresser before fixing himself a drink and joining the argument. And he had left them behind after making his position clear: here was a man who didn't suck up to anybody. *Semper Fi.*

He wondered where he had spent his last sou. He took another drink to help him think. Nothing big. He had come to France with plenty of money knowing that was the only interest foreigners had in Americans. He would call the hotel and ask his wife to bring money. No, he didn't want her coming to a place like this. There wasn't a woman in the bar, although there were two men dressed as women.

He would ask his wife to give money to a cab driver; no, better that she give the money to the concierge. Surely, the concierge would know a reliable driver. He would get the bartender to give the name and address of the bar to the concierge. All he had to do was to explain his situation to the bartender.

He approached the bar and ordered a cognac. "Cognac, number one," he said, holding up a thumb. The gorillas exchanged glances. He did not pick up the drink when it was placed before him; instead, he said slowly and clearly, "Choy oy." It was a Vietnamese exclamation that meant "Oh dear!" or something similar, but it was the only other language he knew. "Choy oy. I don't have any money with me. I left it in the hotel. I wish to call the concierge and ask him to send the money and a cab."

The bartender squinted an eye and canted his head. The thugs leaned closer.

"Con-ci-erge," he said clearly, accenting every syllable. With the forefinger of both hands he pointed at the barkeep. "You call concierge. Tell him to bring money. Francs," he said in his best French. "Boo coo francs." He was better at this than he thought.

The goons crowded around, leaving their stools and chairs to do so, all speaking and gesturing at once. The two men-ladies remained at their table, and in a dark corner an old, scarred brute of a man watched but did not move. "Con-ci-erge," Paul shouted above the din. "You call con-ci-erge. Tel-e-fono con-ci-erge."

The bartender held out one hand in the universal gesture for "pay up" and pointed at the door in the universal signal for "and get out" with the other.

It was clear he needed help. "Parley vouz Français?" he asked. Several echoed the barkeep's answer. "Parley vouz American?" he tried again. He managed to strike them dumb. The shouting and gesturing stopped except for the barkeep, who still held out one hand for payment and one hand for direction. If he couldn't make them understand, he was in Indian country. "Boo coo money hotel," he said. What the hell was the name of the hotel? "Ho-tel La Maison Entraygues," he guessed.

"Eh?" The bartender canted his head more and squinted his eye closed in an effort to understand. The barkeep didn't speak English, and he didn't understand French.

"Te-te money here." He pointed at the place he stood. "Here. Te-te money here." He turned out his empty pocket in the universal language for broke.

The barkeep caught him by the front of the shirt. He knocked the hand away but other hands grabbed him, other arms held him. He suggested a compromise. "Okay, okay. I di-di to La Maison Entraygues, get boo coo francs, come back. Maybe bring con-ci-erge. You understand di-di?" He freed one hand enough to wiggle two fingers in the Indian sign language of a brave hurrying to get wampum.

In the dark corner the hulk rose to his feet. If the French had a mafia, this was the don. If they had a religion, this was the Grand Inquisitor. If they had a navy, this was Captain Bligh. He slowly made his way across the small room until they were face to face. "Di-di?"

"Oui," Paul said in a gesture of peace. "I di-di to La Maison Entraygues. Chop chop. Get my wallet. Billfold. Francs. Boo coo francs. Come back. Pay. Leave big tip. Buy a drink for everyone." Unable to wave a generous hand, he used his chin to include everyone.

Scarface examined him through eyes that were almost filmed. "Di-di?"

"I'm not looking for trouble, but if it comes you're cacad-ow, buddy. I've been in worse places than this in Saigon."

"Saigon?" Scarface repeated like a ravaged parrot.

"Yes. I mean, oui."

"Vietnam?"

The old guy didn't even know where Saigon was. "Oui. Vietnam."

"Vietnam," Scarface said, pounding his chest with a thick hand. "Saigon, oui. Ban Me Thout, oui. Pleiku, oui. Tourane."

Paul remembered that Tourane was the French name for

Da Nang. "Tourane," he said, nodding. He would have poked a finger at his chest but his arms were still being held. "Hoi An. You called it Faifo. Phu Bai. Quang Tri."

"Quang Tri?" The old guy's eyebrows yo-yoed. He pointed at a scar on his face and said, "My Chanh." He threw his arms up and out and then pointed again at the scar. Wounded by an explosion, probably a mine.

"I been through there but didn't spend much time. Hue?"

The old guy grumbled something and Paul's hands and arms were released, his clothing straightened. The old guy shoved the glass of cognac away with the flat of his hand. He spoke again and glasses appeared before them. "Pleiku," he said. He grumbled again, deep in his throat, but no one seemed to understand him this time. He grumbled again. "Ahhh," he said. "Pleiku. Diep."

Paul knew that Diep was a name, sometimes a girl's name. "Diep?" he asked. There was a deep rumble that seemed to come from the bottom of the belly. At least that much was clear.

"An Khe, Kontum, Dak Doa, Plei Rinh." He raised his eyes as though looking up at hills, held up his arms and turned completely around. Surrounded.

"Oui. Pleiku. I've never been there but I know you guys lost a lot of good men in there. Indian country. Bad for ambushes."

"Plei Rinh," the old guy said again. He said something to the others while miming driving with a steering wheel in both hands. He dropped the steering wheel and grabbed a rifle, shooting in all directions. He unbuttoned his shirt to reveal a puckered scar in his side. "Plei Rinh." He fell to his knees, crawled a few paces and curled up on his side.

Paul rolled up a sleeve and pointed at a scar. "Khe Sahn," he said.

"Khe Sahn. No Dien Bien Phu."

No, it wasn't Dien Bien Phu. It never would have been Dien Bien Phu, no matter what the media said. "Hill 881."

The old guy nodded. "It wasn't a bad wound. I didn't want to leave my buddies, you know? They were fighting for their lives and I was drinking beer in Da Nang and watching a movie every night. By the time I got back three of them were dead. Hell, the medevac was worse than the wound. The chopper got hit on the way out and I thought it was going to fall out of the sky."

The old guy nodded and grunted. Paul looked at the ruffians; they nodded and sighed too, although most of them were too young to have been in Vietnam.

Paul pulled up his trouser leg to show another scar. "Dai Loc. Grenade." He turned the back of his hand. "Saigon," he said. That scar had come the last night of his first tour when he was permitted his first look at Saigon. He had gotten in a fight with a Saigon commando who pushed pencils at Tan Son Nhut Airport during the day and shacked up with a Vietnamese woman at night. Paul hadn't known that at the time. He just knew that she was a Vietnamese woman who spoke English and he hadn't talked to a woman since R&R. Instead of confronting Paul, the commando had slapped the woman and Paul had punched the guy. He didn't know the guy was with three buddies. He hadn't won that fight but he hadn't exactly lost it either.

"Saigon," the old guy said, putting an arm around Paul's shoulder. "Gia Dinh."

"Oui," Paul said. He had spent only one night in Saigon but he knew Gia Dinh was almost a suburb.

The old guy said a few words in French and then "Tien," another name. The others murmured, chuckled, nodded their heads.

"Saigon dinky dow," Paul said, approximating the Vietnamese expression for crazy.

The old guy said something to the toughs, who broke into laughter and clapped both of them on the back. Paul was among friends. He picked up his glass, said, "Vive la France," and drained it.

"Vive la France," the others shouted as more drinks appeared before him. "Vive America."

"Vive Vietnam," the old guy said in a voice that came close to tenderness. "Vive Kontum. Vive Pleiku. Vive Plei Rinh." He dropped his head over his drink. Paul feared the old guy was going to get maudlin. Then he raised his head and his glass and said, "Vive Diep."

The room exploded with shouts and more drinks appeared. The bartender did not appear to be keeping count. Neither was Paul.

"I better get back to my hotel," Paul said while he could still talk. "Hotel La Maison Entraygues." His French seemed to be improving.

The old guy put his hands on Paul's shoulders and kissed his cheeks. "Mon frere," he said. "Mon frere."

Paul wasn't sure of the meaning but he knew he had met a comrade. He repeated the words as best he could. The Frenchmen chuckled and shook their heads, then drank to "les freres."

"I have to get back to my hotel," Paul said. "Hotel La Maison Entraygues." They looked at each other without understanding but nodded solemnly, waiting for the signal to toast his favorite cause. "I'm tired. Go to sleep now." He placed his palms together beside his head and rested his head upon them. They murmured solemnly and raised their glasses in the universal gesture of brotherhood with the dead.

"My wife is waiting," Paul explained. "She'll be worried. Wife. Fille. Woman." He shaped curves with his hands. They grunted, sighed, groaned, rolled their eyes and raised their glasses in the primal toast to life's complexity.

Dawn was breaking when he staggered from the bar, buoyed by goodwill, maintained by the need to appear erect and composed when he returned to his room. The desk clerk eyed him with studied insolence and pretended not to understand when he asked for a key to his room. Paul smiled and clapped him on the shoulder. Upstairs, he tapped gently at his door. His wife opened it immediately and followed him into the room.

"Are you okay?" she asked. "Where have you been? I've been worried sick."

"I'm sorry," he said. "I didn't mean to worry you. I . . . I ran into some friends and . . . lost track of time. I left my watch here."

"You left your billfold too. What did you do?"

"I ran into a . . . buddy. From Vietnam." It had happened before, someone he could talk to. Who understood without speech, just an occasional name or glance or punch on the arm to show they were thinking the same thoughts, remembering similar places and events. Sometimes such meetings lasted only minutes. Sometimes they lasted for hours while he forgot his wife, his career, his commitments, lost in memories and feelings that he could rarely share.

"Please don't walk out like that," his wife said. "No matter where we are."

"I won't," he promised and meant it.

"I won't ask you to travel with me again."

"I want to come back here sometime. But not like this. I want to live with the people. Drink wine with them. Learn a little of their language, their ways."

"I won't ask you to sit with those people again."

"I'll sit with anyone you want to sit with," Paul said magnanimously. What the hell? "I'll even be polite."

"Would you, Paul?" she asked, putting her arms around him. "Because they're people I think we'd like to know. I think they could help us in our careers, both of us."

He kissed her. She was his wife, the woman he loved and wanted to live with always. But he knew she would never understand him the way he was understood by an old man who had been wounded by the Viet Minh and left in the bushes to die. He thought he had been working without a net but his was stronger than hers. *Semper Fi.*

Defender of the Faith

As a child I believed in all the abstractions. Purity. Honor. Love. I was in love with Joy McKinney, who was a couple of inches taller and almost a year older than I. In eighth grade, our first year in high school, being in love meant that I carried her books, we ate lunch together and sat together on the bus. We watched "Leave it to Beaver" at her house and read Archie comic books at mine. I gave her my Boy Scout scarf and she gave me the silver unicorn pin her grandmother had given her on her fourteenth birthday. "But it was a birthday present," I protested.

"I'm too old for unicorns," she said. "I wanted a ticket to the Elvis Presley concert."

I loved Joy McKinney as truly, as purely as I loved my mother. I dreamed of rescuing her from sorcerers and defending her from dragons. Nothing could defeat pure love, not even a witch's curse. The movies, the magazines, the song writers said so. Even the minister said love could overcome the world, or something like that.

But there were no sorcerers or dragons in the high school boys' room, just Troy Bingham. "I hear you popped Joy McKinney," one of the older boys said to Troy. Troy was on the football team, maybe one of the backs.

"Yeah."

"What did you do?"

"We were sitting on her porch talking and I started feeling her up."

"Didn't she tell you to stop?"

"She told me." They all laughed at that and crowded in closer. "When I got my hands between her legs she said if I didn't stop she was going to call her father. I said, 'He'll come out here and kill both of us.' After that she kind of gave up."

"And you made her?"

"Naw, I kissed her goodnight."

They were laughing and hooting and I wormed my way through them, screamed "Liar," and flailed at Troy. He seemed more surprised than anything else. I wanted to smash his face and I would have if I could. He grabbed my hands and shoved me against the wall. "What's the matter with you?" he asked.

"Maybe he's her boyfriend," someone said.

"Him? He hasn't even got hair yet."

"Let's see if he has hair." They pulled down my jeans and underpants and pointed and laughed, leaving me sobbing. When I looked up, I saw Petey from one of my classes. "What happened?" he asked.

I fastened my pants and blew my nose with one finger, trying to hide the tears. "I had a fight with Troy Bingham."

"Are you okay?"

"Sure." I spat in a urinal.

"What did you fight about?"

"He lied about Joy and I hit him."

Petey was smarter than I thought. His eyes widened in recognition. "They did it, didn't they?" He made it sound like a personal triumph.

"He lied. Troy lied," I yelled after him, but, empowered by imagination, Petey ran to tell others.

I avoided people the rest of the day, but I could see them looking at me. I was the crybaby, the kid. I saw them looking at Joy too, whispering about her. I wanted to defend her but I was kept at bay by their sharp tongues and glittering eyes.

I sat beside Joy on the bus after school, too wretched to look her in the eye. She had been humiliated, shamed, and I had done nothing to help her. "What is it? What's wrong?" she asked when we got off the bus. I looked down the street. There were no dragons, no pits, no lairs, just neat lawns around neat houses with picture windows. I didn't deserve to walk her home. I should have met Troy after school. Even if I couldn't hurt him, I should have fought him. "It's Troy, isn't it?" she asked.

"We had a fight," I said, hoping she hadn't heard that Troy laughed at me and pulled down my pants.

"I want you to leave Troy alone. You're just going to get hurt."

I didn't care if I got hurt. I wished Troy had hit me, had blackened an eye or knocked out a tooth, something honorable. I should have fought him until he admitted he lied, no matter how much he hurt me. Joy was the best person I knew. I should have defended her before the whole school.

"It wasn't right what Troy did to you," she said. "Well, to me either."

Something dark had happened. Something unaccountable. "Joy. . . ."

"I didn't mean to hurt you."

I looked at her then. I had to look up; she was taller than I. What I saw wasn't anger or hurt but something new, something I had never seen before. "You didn't let him?"

"We went for a walk. We talked for a while. He is so mature, he knows so much about things I hadn't even thought about."

"What things?"

"Just things, you know. He liked me. I could tell that. He listened to me."

"I listen to you."

"I know, but this is . . . he's different. He . . . he understands me. He knows what I'm feeling."

"I like you."

"I know, but. . . . I don't know how to make you understand."

"Understand what?"

"Things are different, Billy. It's not the way you think it is."

"What isn't?"

"The world isn't. Let's not talk about it anymore."

We had already started toward her house and I walked with her, guiding her around the water sprinklers. I knew that it wasn't Joy's fault. I could scarcely believe that boys did things like that to hurt girls. I wanted her to know that I would never have done anything like that to her, never have caused her shame or disgrace. Never. And I would see to it that no one else did again. Together we could beat Troy Bingham and people like him. "I'm going to kill him."

"Billy, stop it."

Once I said it, I knew I could do it. "My father has a shotgun," I said. "I've shot it before."

She stopped and turned to face me. "Billy, it wasn't like you think. He made me feel. . . ."

She didn't have the words to explain her feelings and I didn't have the feelings to understand her words. "Did you kiss him back?"

"I did whatever he wanted. It wasn't all his fault. He wasn't mean or anything. He said he was sorry. I know what he did to you wasn't right but I want you to forget about it and not have any more trouble with him."

"I don't want you to have to see him every day, to be in the same school with someone like that."

"Billy, I'm going to see him again."

"If I kill him, you won't ever have to face anyone like that again."

"I'm going to see him tonight."

I was stunned, bewildered beyond comprehension. What happened to love? And trust, and forever? If those words didn't mean anything, then what did? She looked at me, I think, with sadness. "You're such a child," she said.

"I'm not a child," I said, although my eyes stung. "What makes you so grown-up?" She didn't answer. "What about the pin you gave me?"

"You can keep it," she said.

"I don't want it now." I watched her walk away and tried to imagine her walking with Troy. Holding the hand that had forced her. Not in my world. "I'm going to flush it down the toilet," I yelled.

I didn't though. I took a hammer and beat the pin to pieces. Then I looked at my comic books until Mother told me to turn out the light. The next day was Saturday but I didn't call Joy or go by her house. I played war with the younger kids. They asked me if I had ever kissed a girl. I told them I had a girlfriend but that I liked dogs better.

Three days later I saw my first hippie. He was from California and he was barefooted, long-haired and wore a dirty T-shirt and torn jeans. He was sent home to shave, get a haircut and dress properly for school.

The next year an invasion failed at the Bay of Pigs. Two years later I watched John Glenn orbit the earth and police dogs prevent children from going to school. I saw an assassin shot on television. Two years after that I was in Vietnam fighting for freedom. Then a year in California rioting for peace. Followed by self-realization in college, oneness in marriage and fulfillment in a career.

Three years after marriage I found forever in a son. Who died when he was eight. The next year my wife left for self-discovery. Two years after that I was replaced by the boss' daughter-in-law for sexual equality.

I went back to school for success. I married a twenty-five-year-old woman with a five-year-old daughter for happiness. Four years later, my wife left to find community, taking her daughter with her. Yesterday I was passed over for promotion, no longer part of the company's future. I have security but there will be no surprises, no stars, no rainbows.

At a class reunion I learned that after high school Joy went to work at an insurance company and married one of the salesmen. They had three children. One of her sons was a salesman like his father. One daughter was a housewife who sold Avon products. One daughter was a career soldier. I learned this when I told Joy who I was.

"Did we get drunk together?" she asked.

"No, we read Archie comic books."

"Were you on the football team?"

"That was Troy Bingham," I said and watched as she remembered him.

"He was a back."

"I once had a fight with him because of you," I said.

"Were we ever that young?"

"I was."

"Do you ever see him?"

"I see him everywhere I go."

She seemed puzzled by that, even suspicious. "Who won the fight?"

"He won but I didn't run."

"Then you didn't lose."

"No, I didn't lose."

"Why did you fight him?"

There was little about her of the Joy I remembered. The Joy who laughed at Veronica and Betty, who said I was making things worse when I attacked dust motes with a wooden sword. "I was defending something."

"What?"

I didn't answer her. I thought it was to save embarrassment to both of us. A year later I realize I didn't answer because I didn't know. If I knew, I could believe in unicorns again.

Volunteers

He had seen her kind in every bar from Dallas to Da Nang. A wife too soon, a mother too young, a divorcee too late — after her face and worth had been altered. Somewhere there was a child, probably with an aunt or grandmother, while she worked the bar at night and took classes by day, trying to escape the life she had volunteered for.

He had been a volunteer too, and was trying to escape his pain in the same bar, although he didn't have to smile and flirt to pay for books and baby-sitting. He earned his recompense painting over graffiti on restroom walls, repairing ill-used dorm rooms and replacing light bulbs and window panes in classrooms where he was as anonymous as the decor. That's where he had first seen her — sitting in the empty classroom, head on her desk. He had thought she was asleep, and he was going to tell her to clear out so he could work, but when he saw she was crying he left her alone. He had seen enough crying women to last a lifetime.

"How's school?" he asked her when she came to his table.

"Okay," she said, saving the smile for tipping customers. "What can I get you?"

After ordering a beer, he leaned back and examined the photographs and posters that decorated the wall. He too had been decorated by another's design. In the background, the stereo played a song about the words of the prophets being written on tenement walls. Was that what he was doing, painting over the words of the prophets?

~

He had seen her kind on every campus from Ann Arbor to Austin, big eyes, big ears, big tits. Somewhere there was a mother who hosted the Women's Missionary Society and a father who was past president of Kiwanis. He, too, had fled that kind of poverty for the richness of academic life. He had first seen her in his classroom, lingering after the bell rang. He had thought she wanted to complain about the assignment and he had ignored her. He had seen enough of those to last a lifetime. Then he found she had read his book. She thought he was wise and experienced, and she wanted to be near him, to hang on his words, to learn all he knew.

She was flattered that a man of his intelligence found her attractive. He was flattered that a woman of her youth found him exciting. They were both flattered that on campus or in the bar, they were subjects of gossip and speculation.

"This is such a neat place," she said. "I've never been in a place that's just so — so real."

It was a decorator's dream of the sincere sixties. The walls were covered with crude posters urging "Make Love Not War" and "Burn Baby Burn"; caricatures of Johnson and Nixon; photographs of John and Robert Kennedy, Martin Luther King, Che Guevara, Ho Chi Minh, Malcolm X, Bobby Seale, Janis Joplin, and Maharishi Mahesh; paraphernalia from head shops; and old uniforms — headbands, love beads, fringed leather jackets, dashikis, Nehru jackets, strategically torn jeans. In the background, Peter, Paul and Mary sang "Blowing in the Wind."

"I hoped you'd like it," the professor said. He had brought women here before, students mostly. It made them feel daring and a little rebellious to be in a theme bar with an older man. "Listen to this song." Over the music of "Silent Night" was the radio announcement of anti-black riots, the death of Lenny Bruce and Richard Nixon calling for a stepped-up effort in Vietnam.

"It's like being a part of history," she said.

He masked his fear of the day when this place and that time marked him not as exciting and experienced but as old and amusing. "I was young, but I remember it. I remember seeing Lee Harvey Oswald die, and the Kennedys, and Buzz Aldrin on the moon. I remember the Beatles on the 'Ed Sullivan Show.' "

"You have seen so much."

"I have been through a lot," he admitted.

He had overheard students speaking of the bar with awe, a place where they could mingle with professors, listen to the music and pretend they were part of the days of rage, righteousness and glory. He listened to the stereo — a song about pills and feeding your head. He didn't need the waitress to tell him he was out of place. Still, he sat alone at his table, listening to the music, trying to understand.

"What's that?" he asked as the music changed.

"I think that's the Grateful Dead, or maybe the Mothers of Invention. I don't know, that's your generation, not mine."

Maybe it was his generation but the music was as foreign to him as the posters. "How do you like working in a place like this?" he asked, referring to the theme, not the job.

"I've got a son, five and a handful," she said. "What do you expect me to do, brain surgery?"

The only job she could get, and no matter what life offered her, she would never leave the kid. Women were like that. He had deserted the children. Even though he hadn't understood at the time that was what he was doing, he had left them.

⁂

"What was it like?" the student asked. "It must have been exciting to know that you were taking part in something historic."

"I remember one demonstration," the professor said, suggesting that he was choosing one of many. He had been exempted from the draft and he was too busy pursuing grades and scholarships to pay much attention to the war. It was there and he was opposed. Like other students, he knew the right words to say about it, and about the soldiers, police and president. "We brought traffic to a standstill. They called out the police, the Highway Patrol, the National Guard. I'll never forget the smell of tear gas."

"I've never been a part of anything important," she said.

He had been a part, for a little while. One day, tired of studying, he had left the library to see what all the noise was about. A crowd had gathered around a burning car that blocked an intersection. He had been fascinated by a young woman who taunted the authorities, and he watched the careless, unconscious way she walked, and tossed her hair. He had been entranced by the danger and the openness and togetherness of the protesters. When the protest was disrupted by tear gas and nightsticks he had run with the others, happy to be one of them. The defiant young woman had caught his hand and he had allowed her to guide him.

For a while they had lived together. Strangers ran in and out of the apartment, lay around, smoked dope, shouted into the telephone and cranked the mimeograph machine while he tried to study. She had given herself the name of a Hindu god, a name he could never remember, and was into what she called "guerrilla theater." She and her friends put on makeup and weird costumes and portrayed napalmed peasants, manacled slaves, dispossessed Indians or the ravaged earth. Mostly she was into ecology and the environment. She wanted him to follow her to a commune where they would write poems and grow grass, but she was just too weird.

"I wish I had been alive then. It was so exciting," the student said.

He had thought the world sucked. "What I remember is the music."

"And the tear gas," she reminded.

"Yes, the tear gas."

~

"What's your son's name?"

"Billy."

"I bet he's a good kid."

"Yes, he's a great kid, and let me save you some time. I don't date customers. I go to school, I go to work, I take care of my boy, and I do not intend to drag a lot of men through his life. Maybe someday he'll have a father and I'll have a husband, but right now I'm the only parent he's got and the only important thing is what happens to him."

What had happened to the kids? That's what he had never been able to get out of his mind. He had spent three years in a little ville on the Song Thu Bon and had volunteered for a fourth but the Marines sent him home because he was getting too tight with the civilians. Although he had been planning a military career, he had taken his discharge, intending to go back to the ville, but before he had money for a plane ticket, the North Vietnamese overran the whole country. After that he had no plans. He had drifted, working at odd jobs, but he had never made a beginning.

He sat in bars wondering what had happened to the old mamasans who planted the pumpkin seeds he gave them, tended the pigs sent by a Future Farmers of America Club in Nebraska and cried when he left. What had happened to the papasans who knew nothing about soldiering but carried rifles to defend their homes and accompanied the Marines on patrols and ambushes?

But it was the kids he couldn't forget. He had taught them to play football. He had given them Christmas presents sent by groups in the States, things they had never seen before — Frisbees, baseball gloves, toy trains and fire trucks. Once someone had sent them a record labeled "California Dreamin'," but there were no stereos in the ville, no electricity, no time for listening to music. He had taught them to shoot the M-16 and throw grenades.

Where were they now, those children who knew so much of war? At peace in their ville? In prison? Raped, killed or kidnapped by pirates? Had some of them made it to the States? He didn't know where to look and there was no way they could find him. They had always been a world apart. Even when they lived in the same ville they had been a world apart.

"What were you protesting?" the student asked.

He couldn't remember exactly what the demonstration was over; perhaps he had never known. There had been so many issues — the war, black power, student rights, the diversion of resources from teaching to military research, saving the condor, the redwoods, the whales. "The main thing," he said and stopped himself because he had almost said "they." "The main thing we were protesting was the abuse of authority."

"Power and its legitimation," she said. "I read your book."

"It wasn't just the federal government. Universities thought they could demand anything of students. Everything was a hassle."

"It hasn't changed. It took me three hours to get through registration because I didn't want to take P.E."

"Getting a doctorate was pure hell." He shook his head at the memory. The director of his dissertation was pirated by another university, and his new director would not approve his thesis or subject after he had done the outline and had almost completed the research and first draft. "They threw out my research and told me to start over. I freaked out. I was stoned for a week, trying to decide whether to commit suicide or homicide. I almost dropped out. Then I thought of the investment of time and money I had made. I started over again, but it was hell." He had almost gotten a divorce. His wife thought he had failed his chance and now it was her turn.

"Hey, Mabel," he yelled. "How about some service? A man could die of thirst in here." The student giggled.

The waitress hurried to their table. "I'm sorry," she apologized to the student, "but I'm going to have to card you."

"I'm old enough," the student said.

The professor put his arm around the waitress. "Honey," he said, "when a girl's old enough to say yes, she's old enough to drink."

"I'm sorry," the waitress said. "I don't care what people do, but it's the law, and if the cops came in here this place could lose its license, and I'd lose my job."

The student dug in her purse and pulled out her driver's license and handed it to the waitress. "Some people just like to show their authority," she said.

He listened to a song about a nowhere man, sitting in a nowhere land, making nowhere plans for nobody. That's who he was. Nowhere man. He could spend the rest of his life painting over graffiti and no one would ever know he was there. "Do you ever listen to the words, Mabel?" he asked when she brought another beer. She passed him every day on the campus and didn't know who he was.

"I don't have time for listening. And my name's not Mabel."

"I thought the professor called you Mabel."

She shrugged. "It's just something to call me. I was in his class last semester but he doesn't recognize me."

She too was invisible, an interchangeable, recyclable piece of the furniture of their lives, noted only when absent.

"Was it as wild as everybody says? The parties, the drugs?"

"The whole society was uptight. Everything was a confrontation whether you were asking your parents for money, or the school for curricular changes, or whatever. Whenever we got a chance, we wanted to turn on, lay back and groove on the music."

"Everything used to be freer, more fun," she said. "Now there is so much competition. All anybody cares about is making grades and making money."

"You should try being on the faculty. Just try to get tenure some day. I did all the shit work the tenured professors refused to do. I tutored, advised, served on every damn useless committee they could dream up, sponsored clubs and fraternities, taught extra classes without pay, and then they said none of that counted unless I got my book published. And you know what they said when I got a publisher? They wished I had taken time to find a more prestigious press. If I had waited three more months I would have been out on my ass."

He leaned back in his chair, exhaled heavily trying to blow away his anger and frustration and yelled, "Mabel."

"I really admired your book," she said. "I never understood contemporary colonialism, nationalism, stratification and social control on the international level until I read your book. I had never understood how Americans could be war criminals."

"It wasn't just governmental criminal behavior," he said. "There was political and corporate criminal behavior. And there was the Silent Majority. Given the social interaction between the decision-makers and bureaucratic organizations, you can understand how soldiers could slaughter entire villages in Vietnam."

"Vietnam" split the space between their tables like an

RPG, hung in the air like a flare, whistled in his ear like a mortar, linked them like the chain of command. He didn't want to be aware of them. He didn't want to be part of their lives, to hear their conversation, but it was as inescapable as defeat.

The professor shook his head. "It was too horrible to describe."

What was too horrible to describe? It was too monotonous to describe. It was too miserable to describe. He didn't know the horror until he came home.

"They were killing peasants who had done nothing except try to defend their homes."

He set down his beer and turned to stare at them. Everyone had something to say about the war but the vets, and if they didn't speak up, no one would ever know what it was like. But where to begin? "I was there," he said.

They stiffened a little but pretended not to hear him. He was as invisible in the bar as he had been on the campus. They didn't want to hear him, but if he couldn't make them listen, how could the truth ever be known?

"I was there," he said, louder this time. He had to be careful. Once before he had tried to straighten someone out and there had been a fight. Well, hardly a fight. Pushing mostly, but chairs had been knocked over, bottles broken. Although no one was hurt, it had made headlines. Vietnam veteran goes berserk in barroom brawl. "I may not know everything that happened, but I know enough to know you don't know shit."

The professor turned, bringing the full weight of his doctorate to bear. "I wrote a book, *The Sociology of Wars of Liberation*," he said. "I have read more volumes on Vietnam, examined more documentation — "

"You're full of shit."

The waitress was at his side. "I'm sorry," she said. "If you don't behave you're going to have to leave."

Not until he sank back in his chair did he realize he was trembling. He looked at the door, knowing he ought to get out. It looked a mile away across a mine field of knowing eyes and hidden smiles. And it looked like running. That's what had started the other fight, when he tried to walk away and was accused of being a coward. A coward and a loser. He took a deep breath, picked up his beer and drank.

"I don't know why you let people like that in here," the professor said. "This used to be a place where you could sit and talk without being hassled by people who have no business being in here."

"I'm sorry," the waitress said. "If he gives you any more trouble he's going to leave."

When the waitress left, he tried to recapture the glow that had been torn from the conversation. He hated interruptions. Just when he was about to make a point there was always an interruption. A student came in late or asked a question or —

She patted his hand and smiled at him over her drink. "What's the name of that song?" she asked.

" 'God on Our Side.' " He stared at the intruder, not certain that his prestige had been restored. "Let him fight his war somewhere else," he said loudly to be overheard.

"The war is over," she said, trying to soothe him.

"Not for some people. Some people are never happy unless they have something to fight about." He could have enlisted. He had even considered it to escape the drudgery of his studies. He could have been an officer, but it would have put him four or five years behind his age group on the career ladder.

"Let's forget him. He doesn't matter."

"I'm willing to fight, but it has to be for something. Your right to come in this bar, or any bar, without being hassled by strangers. Your right to have a drink. To have an abortion. Dress any way you like. Pursue any career you choose. I'll fight for that."

"Ready for another beer?"

He wasn't, but he ordered one anyway to avoid being asked to leave.

"Were you really in Vietnam?" the waitress asked. "I guess you know a lot about drugs."

There were drugs in Vietnam — like music, it was in the rear. In the ville they had no barbed wire, no bunkers. They had to depend on their wits, and on each other. Everything he knew about drugs he had learned on the campus.

"My husband — ex-husband — was into drugs. I put up with him lying, being out all night, losing his job, stealing from his parents. When he started taking the kid's milk money I knew I had to get out. You must have seen guys like that."

"No."

"I just want someone to help me understand how getting high could be so important that you'd let your own child go hungry. Throw your wife out in the street. I had a kid, no job skills, nowhere to go for help. How could he do that?"

"I don't know," he said, and he didn't, although he had done something very similar. He had earned their trust. He had convinced them that he would defend their village, that he would lead them to a better life. Then he had come home, leaving them to flee in leaky boats, to starve or drown, be raped, killed, enslaved by pirates, interned in disease-ridden camps.

"Sometimes I think if I could just understand — " she said. Abruptly she walked away.

That had been the ultimate surrender. And the ultimate victory. That he no longer had to understand the walls he painted over.

~

"My parents want me to major in business or computer science so I can make a lot of money," she said.

"I should have gone into business; I know that now. When I think of all I went through to get a doctorate and then seven more years just to get tenure. With the same investment, I would have earned a lot more money."

It had cost him his family too. They had met in graduate school, but when her folks found out they were living together they wouldn't support her anymore. They couldn't live on what his folks were sending, so he married her and she dropped out and got a job. He promised when he got his Ph.D. he would go to work and she could get hers, but the only school that offered him a position had no graduate program in her field. She decided to have a baby instead. He begged her, he pleaded with her to wait until he had tenure. She waited two years while he cowered before administrators, truckled to the wishes of senior professors and fawned over his students seeking to gain advantage over his peers, then she decided her Ph.D. was more important than he was. That had almost cost him tenure. The college expected stability in junior faculty.

"I know I want to make a lot of money, but I want to make it doing something interesting," she said.

"It doesn't get interesting until you get to the top," he said. "If you're not a full professor you're a piece of filth. You don't have any control until you're at least a chair. That's what you have to remember — you have to get to the top before you have any choice."

"I think I want to have a family too."

Another woman who wanted it all. Just like his ex-wife. "When you were growing up, who was the most important person in the family? You were. If you have a family, who is going to be the most important person? Unless you can say that you are, you have no business having a career and a family."

"I've seen you at the college," he said when the waitress came back. "I work there. Carpenter's assistant." Still she said nothing. "What are you studying?"

"Education. I want to be an elementary school teacher. I just think if you can get hold of kids when they're young and show them what's possible — I just didn't know my choices when I was young. I didn't know there were other possibilities."

"So you study with the professor?"

"Just one class. Sociology of the Family. He knew his stuff, kept the class interesting. I just didn't like it. When I studied for the final I went through my notes, and as soon as I memorized a page, I tore it out of the notebook and threw it in the fire. My mother thought I was crazy, but I wanted to forget it as soon as the exam was over. Everybody was — everything was an issue. It was like — " She shrugged.

"I saw you in the classroom one day. You were crying."

"I just get so angry with men. Everything is so easy for them. My husband — ex-husband — asked me for money. He's supposed to be helping support our son and he asks me for money. My mother tried to tell me about him, but he's basically a nice guy. He's just so messed up."

"So you sent him the money."

"It's not the money, it's just so hopeless. And to watch him sliding down a hole like that and not be able to help. My mother says everybody asks for the hell they get. I should have run the first time he looked at me like that. I guess now you wish you had run to Canada."

He had no more thought of Canada than she had thought of running from that look. A brand new high school diploma, no job, no plans for college, his hormones had responded exactly like hers. They had leaped for joy.

"It wouldn't be so hard if I didn't remember how it was and think that there must have been some way I could have saved it," she said.

He remembered it as being where he was supposed to be, doing what he was supposed to do. It was only after he came home that he was depressed, that he knew the horror of what he had left behind, that his folks, his friends looked at him as though afraid he was going to tell them something they didn't want to hear.

"I lived in a ville with the Vietnamese. I made friends with them. I helped them to protect their ville. I taught the kids to play football and throw a Frisbee. I felt good about what I did. Hell, it was the only good thing I've ever done. Then I left, and I haven't felt good about anything since. I had hope in the war. Peace is hell."

"It's not as complicated as it seems," the professor said. "Do you want to be a parent or do you want to be a person?"

"Why can't I be a parent and a person?"

"I don't make the rules, I just try to understand how they operate. Mabel," he called. "Mabel, why are you working in a place like this?"

"It's the only way I can take care of my son and go to school. I want to be sure he has a better chance than I had," she said.

"Isn't that what your parents said? They gave up their life so that you would have a better chance, and you gave up your life so that your son will have a better chance, and he'll give up his life for his children, and nobody will break the cycle or do anything with their own life."

"I'm doing the best I can," the waitress said and walked away.

The professor looked at the student and raised his eyebrows.

"I never thought of it that way before," she said. "But life would be so lonely without a family."

"It can be awfully empty without a career. Look at our working-class hero over there."

"There's so much to decide," she protested.

"Had you rather be a sparrow or a snail? That's why you go to college. It not only helps you make choices, it gives you four more years to make up your mind."

The professor and the girl had left, and he was glad because that meant he could leave too. He hadn't meant to stay so long. He just wanted to see the place and have a beer and try to figure out what it all meant and where it had all gone. "Don't mean nothing," he thought, the expression coming back to him over all the years. "It ain't real."

Once that had been enough, but no more. He had put off thinking long enough. Now he needed some answers. Once he thought he was going to save the world. And then democracy. And then the ville. At least the children. He hadn't even saved himself. He was just another wall to write on.

He looked through his billfold, selected a five and handed it to the waitress. "Buy the kid a toy," he said.

Behind him the Beatles sang that all that was needed was love.

Armistice

Reluctant Truth

I often wonder why I'm not more content. Then I'd be more like my sister and, God, I'd hate to be like her, even if she is pretty and well liked. And I wouldn't be sitting here with my clothes packed so as to be ready to leave home when I'm eighteen and free. I don't think you're really free until you're eighteen and free to leave home. I told Mama, I'm blowing out the candles and then I'm blowing. Ten more months.

I don't mean to say I'm exactly having a blast right now, stuck in my room with a pack of cigarettes while Sabrina is out with Stiles Bridges. And the worst of it is that I'll have to ask Sabrina how the movie ended. Rock Hudson had just had this big argument with the girl he loved and was trapped in a cellar with the girl he hated, and I had to tell Dinky

Meachum, "Take me home right now, Rock Hudson makes me sick." I could hardly say I had to be in at ten when my younger sister could stay out with Stiles Bridges until midnight. Just because I took off my sweater.

Mama says boys don't mind dating a girl who has to be in at ten on Saturday night. Ain't that a crock of proverbial excrement? I had to give Dinky certain concessions because he was taking me home early and I couldn't defend myself energetically because I was supposed to be sick. Why don't parents think of these things?

I can do anything I want but I have to do it before ten o'clock. Sabrina can't do anything — she has been perfect her whole life and God knows if she will ever change — but she has until midnight to do it. Mama believes in protracted morality and Sabrina keeps time by Mama's clock. No hose before thirteen, no lipstick before fourteen, no car dates before fifteen, no going steady before sixteen, sex after marriage and alcohol over her dead body. I think freedom is the interim between puberty and marriage, but Mama believes that's the pregnant pause.

Sabrina is extremely gullible. She believes whatever Mama says when she knows Mama has never been out of the state of Texas. Sabrina wears frilly dresses halfway to her ankles because Mama says she looks sweet in them. She brushes her hair one hundred strokes every night because Mama says boys will respect her for it. She makes straight As in school because Mama says brains are a girl's most attractive feature. She doesn't eat caramel candy because Mama says it will make her face break out. Sabrina's face wouldn't break out if she ate hand grenades.

Sabrina has this dream boat, Stiles Bridges, hanging on her heels, and she complains about how much trouble he is. When he asked her to sit on his side of the car, she told him she promised Mama she'd always keep her seat belt fastened. I'd wrestle an alligator if he looked like Stiles Bridges. Dinky has curly hair and dandruff in his eyebrows, but I respect him a lot. Dinky is drummer in a group called Great Expectations Plus the Living Desert.

Sabrina sings in the choir and has blond hair and blue eyes, and — in her white robe — everyone thinks she is an angel. I have bright red hair and a complexion that has been unfavorably compared to pizza. I have always been taller than anyone in my class. In grade school, for our class picture, I had to stand at the back of the room beside the teacher. I had to stoop to write on the blackboard. I couldn't get my knees under my desk and had to sit with them sticking up on either side. Whenever I told someone what grade I was in they thought I was dumb as hell. Sabrina walked to school on the other side of the street so as not to call attention to herself.

The only time I felt good about my height was when I was the Statue of Liberty at the high-school talent show. I held a torch as the statue and these other girls depicting the Four Freedoms danced around me, while Dinky's band played their original song, "Get Down, Abraham." Of course, Sabrina won first place portraying Portia from *The Merchant of Venice*. I was disappointed, but Dinky said Sabrina was a crowd pleaser but I was an independent thinker. He gave me his Willkie button that had been passed down in his family. I respect him a lot.

People refer to me as the "other daughter" and the only thing that kept my birth from being a scandal was Grandpa's red hair. "Her grandpa has red hair," Mama says every time someone wonders how Sabrina and I could have the same parents. We have to take Mama's word for it because whatever color Grandpa's hair was, none of it is left. "You should be proud to have red hair," Mama says. "Red-haired girls almost always grow up to have exceptional personalities." She smiled when she said it, but Mama always smiles.

Mama doesn't smile because she's happy. She smiles because things are so awful she has to smile to bear them. "Norma, don't you think you would look better in church if you spent more time ironing your dress than ironing your hair?" "Vernon, you don't have to mow the lawn for me; it's the neighbors you should think about." If Mama were a picture it would be called "Christian Lady Smiling Through."

Daddy is a big rumpled bear. Mama says I get my size and style from him. Daddy has a weak stomach and can't eat with Mama smiling at him. He will get up from the breakfast table, make a face, grumble and go mow, with Mama smiling after him.

"Vernon, you don't have to go to church if you don't want to. I'll raise the children by myself." Smile, smile. Daddy will drop the paper and growl, make noises all through church, be cross at dinner and raise hell the rest of the day. Daddy is a Christian every day but Sunday.

The only one Mama can't boss around is her father. " 'y God, don't be smiling at me. I'm old enough to be your father," Grandpa says. Grandpa came to live with us when Grandma died. He sits in his stained white shirt and khaki pants with Grandma's old fuzzy house slippers on his feet and a dirty Stetson on his bald head, spits tobacco in the coffee can Mama puts on the floor and makes ugly remarks about me. " 'y God, that's a tall gal. I believe there's some giraffe in that one."

He deliberately got tobacco juice on my English theme which was on the floor because it was due the next day and I put it in the doorway so I would remember to take it. Miss Mafferty counts off a letter grade if it's even one day late. She gave me a C because of the tobacco stains; she wanted to teach me to be neat like my little sister.

Mama told me to ignore Grandpa, but it's hard to ignore someone who sits at the table gumming his food and saying, " 'y God, I like to see a fat gal eat." I am not fat. Sitting beside Sabrina makes me look fat. Everyone thinks Grandpa is senile but I think he is having the time of his life saying anything he wants to and pretending he's deaf when he doesn't want to hear.

One time I whispered, "There goes Mrs. Wilbanks without a stitch on." Grandpa swallowed his tobacco and started coughing and Mama thought he was having a heart attack. "Don't leave us, Papa, don't leave us," she said, smiling like she was in pain. Sabrina said someone should give Grandpa mouth-to-mouth resuscitation and I knew who she meant but I pretended not to hear. Let her get tobacco stains on her teeth.

Mama thought I was spending too much time with Dinky, and when Sabrina told her I was the Statue of Liberty and the Four Freedoms were drinking, smoking, sex and speech, she practically insisted that I join the Personality Plus Club. "You have so much to offer them." Smile. I didn't want to join because the only people who were members were too fat for Pep Squad, not popular enough for Drama Club and too dumb for Honor Society. Mama thought it was perfect for me.

I only went to one meeting, Initiation Night. Miss Mafferty, our sponsor, left as soon as the pies, cakes and tuna fish sandwiches were gone. There we were, the tallest, fattest, ugliest, dumbest, least popular girls in school trying to have a good time. Opal Marie Schumacker, president of the club and the heaviest person in school — there are persistent rumors that the football coach asked her to play nose guard — pulled out a bottle, said, "Here's to Miss Mafferty," took a gulp and passed the bottle to me.

Tina Benin, who is so nervous she chewed her hair into a page boy, pulled out a pack of cigarettes. Tina was a cheerleader until her nerves broke and she went into a spasm every time she heard a drumroll. She had to drop bookkeeping because when someone punched an adding machine she jumped up and yelled, "Gimme a C." I tapped Tina on the arm to ask for a cigarette and she jumped out of her chair and screamed, "Fight team fight."

I picked up the pack of cigarettes she had dropped, lit one, said, "Here's to Stiles Bridges," took a drink and passed the bottle. Stiles Bridges was captain of the football team so we decided to toast every member of the team. I don't know what we were drinking but it made your tongue want to lay down and die and your stomach jump up and run.

Opal Marie said the more you drank the better it tasted, but it didn't. That's the reluctant truth. I turned to Opal Marie, whose chair had slowly collapsed so that she was half reclining on the floor, and said, "What do you usually do at these meetings?"

"This is it," she said, waving the bottle in her short, stout arm. "Consider yourself initiated."

I took the bottle and initiated myself some more. We smoked and drank and laughed and sang what might have been the club song. I was having a great time until Opal Marie slapped me on the back, breaking my brassiere strap. I had to go to the bathroom and take off my sweater to fix it. I didn't stay long because there was a line of girls outside waiting to be sick.

I don't remember much about going home except that I walked very slowly, partly because I needed time to make up a story and partly because the sidewalk kept wandering out from under me. I decided to tell Mama that some football players had crashed the party and forced us girls to smoke and drink with them. Mama will believe anything about football players if it is bad enough. Daddy was a football player. He wore his football sweater until Sabrina borrowed it for Drama Club car wash. Daddy thought she wanted to wear it.

When I got home I had my story together but I couldn't find the door. Mama came outside and watched me fall off the porch. Sabrina watched too. "Is that Norma? What's the matter with Norma, Mama? Is Norma sick?"

All the time Mama and I were doing our damndest to get me in the house, Sabrina chattered. "Norma's falling into the trellis, Mama. She's got her foot caught in the rose bush, Mama. You've got her arm caught in the door."

When we got into the house, without any help from Sabrina, I made an effort to find the stairs, but Mama led me to a chair. I could tell Mama liked me better as a hypocrite; mothers are someone you protect. "Didn't I tell you something like this was going to happen? Didn't I tell you time and time again?" she said, smiling her tight smile.

I found that hard to deny. My head was sick. My stomach competed for attention. I swallowed and tried to blink away the fuzziness in front of my eyes. The fuzziness was Sabrina. "Oh, Norma, how could you do this to Mama?" Sabrina cried.

I blame this on Sabrina: I leaned back in the chair, crossed my legs and lit a cigarette, burning the end of my nose.

"What are you doing?" Mama asked like she was strangling. Her smile was upside down.

"I'm just smoking this God damn cigarette, Mama. I gather you object," I said, flipping the ashes at Grandpa's spit can.

Mama made little choking noises until she could get her voice back. "Norma, you have been smoking and drinking."

"You're not allowed to smoke at meetings of the Honor Society," Sabrina said.

I swear to God I will kill that girl. I put a hand on my stomach to quell the revolution going on there and began my story. "It was the football team."

"The football team is never invited to Pep Squad parties," Sabrina said.

I will poison her in her sleep. "They weren't invited. They crashed the party. They broke down the door. Mama, it was awful."

I put my head in my hands to keep it from falling to the floor. The stage was set for my story of being forced to smoke and drink — it occurred to me to add dancing because Mama thinks dancing is worse than sex education. I leaned forward to begin, exposing my back to Sabrina.

"Norma, you wore Grandma's cameo to the Personality Plus party," Sabrina said.

Grandma's cameo had been gathering dust on Mama's dresser since Grandma gave it to her the year before she died.

No one wore it or even looked at it. The only reason I took it was because Mama practically made me wear a skirt and sweater when I knew the other girls were going to look as tacky as possible, and I didn't want them to think I thought it was a big honor to be a member. It worked too. Opal Marie said, "That skirt and sweater is kind of funky, Norma, but if you keep wearing that pin, you're just asking to be a virgin."

"Norma, did you have permission to wear Grandma's cameo?" Sabrina asked. "Mama, did you say Norma could wear Grandma's cameo? Norma, why is Grandma's cameo on the back of your sweater?"

It took my fuddled brain just two seconds to figure out what had happened. "I had to take off my sweater," I began, and would have explained except that Sabrina screamed, "In front of the football team? I'll never be Football Queen now." Poisoning her in her sleep is too good for her.

Mama got very calm. Her smile was so tight it stretched the corners of her eyes. "Norma," she said, her mouth looking like a rubber band that had been pulled until it was ready to pop, "you will go upstairs, put your clothes straight, wash your face, and when you come back, you had better be prepared to face your father." The band popped. "Vernon," she screeched.

Daddy's growls rang in my ears as I tried to scale the stairs, which looked as steep as my chances of ever being free. Three or four lunges carried me to the top and I got to the bathroom one second ahead of my stomach contents. Sabrina sat on the side of the tub and passed the time inquiring about my health. "Does your head hurt? Does your stomach feel awful? I think there's a big orange soda pop in the refrigerator. That might settle your stomach. I saw this movie where this alcoholic swallowed raw eggs."

I washed my mouth and examined the strange, waxy face that appeared in my mirror. Giving Grandpa time to find a chair. Grandpa loves family forums.

"Norma, come down where I can see you," Daddy yelled. Daddy thinks if he can't see you, you can't hear him.

I made my way down the stairs, careful not to fall. Mama was sitting on the couch where I would have to sit beside her and listen to her smile crack. Daddy was sitting directly across from the couch, holding a glass of milk in both hands. It upsets Daddy's stomach for Mama to screech.

Grandpa was sitting right at the foot of the stairs so that I had to walk around him. Grandpa always spits right. No matter which way he is looking, he spits right. I got a whiff of his sweet chewing tobacco breath and my stomach turned over.

Sabrina was perched on the arm of Daddy's chair with her arm around his shoulder, like she wasn't the one who complains because Daddy wears his old clothes in the house instead of the robe she gave him last Christmas. Daddy doesn't like new clothes. He puts them in the closet until Mama says, "I'm going to give this to the Salvation Army. You never wear it."

"Norma," Mama said. If she had been a pitcher, you couldn't pour water between her lips. "Tell your father what you have been up to."

I decided Daddy would prefer not to hear about the football team. "Oh, Daddy, it was just awful," I said. "It was Initiation Night."

"At Drama Club initiation you have to recite a speech from Shakespeare without a single mistake," Sabrina said. "Some of the others thought they had to have a cigarette for their nerves but I didn't. That's why they selected me Drama Sweetheart."

Slow torture with a blunt instrument might be appropriate. "One of the girls made up something nasty for us to drink," I said. "It must have had alcohol in it." I could hear Mama's smile crumble. "It was just awful." I made a face. It couldn't be too big a sin if I didn't enjoy it.

"How much did you have?" Mama asked. Mama loves gory details. When I was little I had to tell her what I threw up.

"There was spaghetti, and English peas, and — " "Did you see caramel candy?" "No, Mama, I swear." Mama believed caramel candy caused my face to break out and my teeth to have gaps.

I added up the football players we had been able to name and divided by six. "I only had two drinks."

"Why did you have two if the first was so awful?" Sabrina asked.

When Sabrina was a little girl I tried to bury her in the sandpile under handfuls of sand. I wish I had used the shovel. "It was initiation," I explained. "If I didn't drink it, they wouldn't let me be a Personality Plus."

Dad looked sympathetic. I bet he had been initiated. Mama would have preferred that I let them tear out my tongue. Mama believes Jesus turned wine into water.

" 'y God, I knew a woman that drank," Grandpa said. "Jezebel."

"How did Grandma's cameo get on the back of your sweater?" Sabrina asked. I wish I had used the shovel to bash her brains. "You said something about the football team."

I could hear Mama's smile drumming against her teeth. Daddy slurped milk. "Nothing but a Jezebel," Grandpa shouted. Grandpa loves to get worked up and there's not much he can get excited about anymore. "A whistling woman and a crowing hen always come to some bad end," he whined.

It was a straw and I grabbed at it. "I have never whistled in my life," I said. "Sabrina is the one who whistles. I can't whistle because my teeth are too far apart because Daddy would never buy me braces."

Daddy sat up, catching his sleeve under Sabrina and ripping it off the shirt that Mama refuses to mend anymore. If there's one thing Daddy can't stand it's being called a tightwad just because he wouldn't pay for my braces. Just because we've lived in this same house for twenty years. There are countries that are newer than our house. Nails had just been invented. Bathrooms were still a mystery, which explains why there is only one upstairs. "Go to your room," Daddy said.

I was willing but Mama was not. "Not before she explains about the football team," Mama said.

" 'y God, that gal crowed like a rooster," Grandpa said, caught up in his memory of Jezebel. "One drink, that's all it took."

"Did I say 'football team'? I meant Stiles Bridges and the other captain. They were looking for Sabrina."

Perched on Daddy's chair with her arm around his neck, Sabrina did her impersonation of an organ grinder's monkey, mouth open, eyes big, head turning from side to side. "What did Stiles Bridges want with me?"

I blame myself for this: except for that little fib I might have had a chance with Stiles because Sabrina snubbed him since she was in honors English and he was in a class for those without a native language. "I think they wanted to talk to you about being Football Queen."

Sabrina entranced us with her impersonation of a silent movie star mouthing, "Me." And I thought the Drama Club did nothing but sell caramel candy. There is caramel candy in every room and four boxes in the closet. Sabrina was Drama Club Sweetheart because she sold more caramel candy than anyone in the club.

"Football Queen gets a whole page in the yearbook," Sabrina said in wonderment.

"Said she could call wild turkeys but it'd cost me a drink to make her gobble," Grandpa said.

"Why did you take off your sweater?" Mama asked.

I had exposed Sabrina for the shallow overachiever she was and all Mama could think about was my sweater.

"What about the football team? What about Stiles Bridges?" Sabrina asked.

"Norma, you are never to see that Stiles boy again," Mama said, her smile as cold as a sixth-grade dance.

"Mama, it was Sabrina he wanted to see."

"Mama, it was Norma who took off her sweater. It was Norma who wore Grandma's cameo. You won't let me wear it. You won't even wear it yourself."

"I do not approve of Norma wearing it," Mama said. "Whatever possessed you?"

"When I put on that skirt and blouse they seemed so — " I looked at Daddy slowly tearing off the other sleeve so he could use the shirt for a vest — "so new."

"That makes no sense at all," Mama said.

"Of course it does," Daddy said.

"Vernon, I have long been of the opinion you come from a family of ragpickers."

"Well, you come from a family of snuff dippers."

Mama pretends Grandma didn't dip snuff. I thought Mama and Daddy would get in an argument over ancestry and I could escape, but Grandpa said, "Busted her bra trying to gobble."

"Norma, why did you take off your sweater?" Mama said, and everyone turned and looked at me.

I paused dramatically to give Sabrina a chance to get the milk off Daddy's shirt. "Oh, that. Part of the initiation was that we had to wear our clothes backwards. I really am glad you made me wear a skirt and sweater, Mama, because you should have seen the girls who came in blue jeans with shirts that buttoned down the front. They looked so funny."

I think they were disappointed. That's the reluctant truth. I think they hoped something had happened that they could get provoked about. Not that they weren't provoked already.

After a while Mama got her smile working again. "Well," she said, "I always think it is good for us to have these family discussions. And to make it positive, we must all make resolutions to do better." Mama was beaming now. "Vernon, you must resolve that you will throw away those old clothes and wear the robe that Sabrina gave you last year." Daddy growled. "And you must resolve never again to speak disparagingly of my family as long as my father is living in this house."

Daddy didn't say anything, but he likes Grandpa. Grandpa has promised to leave him Grandma's fuzzy slippers when he dies.

"Norma, you will resolve never to take another drink as long as I am alive. No matter how bad it tastes."

"Yes, Mama," I said, wishing she didn't mention taste. I didn't plan to take another drink no matter how long she lived.

"And you will resolve never again, so long as I am alive, to smoke another cigarette."

"Yes, Mama." With Mama the main thing is that everyone resolve something.

"And Sabrina, you must resolve never to go with Stiles Bridges."

"Mama." Sarah Bernhardt, Helen Hayes, Greta Garbo could not have matched the shocked and outraged look on Sabrina's face.

"Resolve," Mother said.

"If I never become Football Queen it'll be your fault," Sabrina said, turning on me. Katharine Hepburn in *The African Queen*. "And I'll never sell you another box of caramel candy."

"What are you going to resolve?" Daddy asked Mama.

"I resolve to have more of these family get-togethers. I feel ever so much better." Blessing us with a smile as bright as the lights in the girls locker room, she went to bed.

We sat and glared at each other. Sabrina was mad at me because she had to get Daddy to get Mama to let her go with Stiles Bridges so she could be Football Queen. Daddy was mad at me for bringing the family together. I was mad at everybody because my life is never going to change. Only Grandpa was happy. He sat there like he was having the time of his life when he's just marking time.

So here I am in my room, smoking and waiting. I don't

care if I get cancer; after your youth is gone, what's left? Old age. Grandpa is in his room with his hat on spitting and remembering. Daddy is grumbling and molting in his old clothes. Sabrina is shining and surpassing. Mama is smiling through. I'll bet I'm never free of this. I bet this is all life is. That's the reluctant truth.

Flight to Amman

"Hakuna matata," the woman behind the Saudia Airlines desk tells you. "There is no problem." There is a problem. You and your wife are Americans. You have tickets for flights from Nairobi to Jeddah, Jeddah to Riyadh, Riyadh to Amman. You have a schedule. You have an itinerary. You have commitments. But the flight from Jeddah to Riyadh has been canceled. Your geography is imperfect, but you have a vision of a straight line from Nairobi to Jeddah to Riyadh to Amman. Americans love straight lines, but a section of the line is missing.

"Your flight is boarding now," the woman insists. "There is no problem."

It is 3:30 A.M. Nairobi is dark and cool. The passengers, who are supposed to be waiting between lines drawn neatly and exactly on the floor, press against your sides. You are the bottleneck to their future. "How will we get to Amman?" you ask, reasonably.

"There is a flight from Jeddah to Cairo at 9:15 A.M. You will be arriving in Jeddah at 7:00 A.M. Hakuna matata. You will board your airplane now, please."

Cairo is not a straight line. You have no schedule, no itinerary, no commitments in Cairo. "Can we get from Cairo to Amman?"

"Hakuna matata. No problem. You will board your airplane now."

"Wait. Has our flight from Jeddah to Cairo been confirmed?"

"That will be taken care of when you arrive in Jeddah. There is no problem. You will board your airplane now."

There is matata, but no choice. The mass of people who have no schedules, no itineraries, no commitments press you into disorder.

The Saudia airliner is modern and spotless, with pretty stewardesses, and a breakfast of water, orange juice, omelette, sausage, croissant, rolls, cheese, butter, jam and coffee. When you finish breakfast you approach the prettiest stewardess and inform her that you are trying to get to Amman but that your flight to Riyadh has been canceled. Where? Riyadh. She calls another stewardess over. The second stewardess calls a steward. None has heard of Riyadh, the capital of their country.

You fish out your ticket and show them. Oh! Riyadh. When the airplane lands you will see men wearing blue trousers, white shirts and blue ties. They are there specifically to help you. You are relieved. Men in white shirts and ties always give you confidence.

As soon as the airplane touches down you grab your handbags and, dragging your wife, elbow your way off the airplane and onto a large bus that has lifted itself to the height of the airplane cabin. After everyone is aboard, it lowers itself to the tarmac and drives to a huge wall with ports that open to receive you. This glimpse of the future causes you to forget momentarily that you are no longer at the head of the line. Recovering, you push to the door and outrun and out-elbow everyone so that you are first to reach the three men in blue trousers, white shirts and blue ties, standing beside a gate. "We're trying to get to Amman," you gasp. "We want the first flight out of here, any airline, any rerouting. We have a schedule."

The three blue ties listen again. They go into conference. They arrive at a solution. "Please sit. Someone will come."

Should you claim your luggage?

"Please sit. Someone will come." Your wife sits down. You do what you usually do in a crisis. You go to the men's room, not because you are nervous, but because you can foresee critical moments ahead which may require you to act quickly and decisively without the mental split focus of looking for the john.

You return from the men's room, attempting to appear in control of the situation, and see the other passengers passing through the gate to the security check where they are separated. The men are publicly frisked; the women are taken one at a time into a large steel cabinet where they are privately frisked. You grab your wife and head for frisking.

"Please sit. Someone will come."

You explain that there is a 9:15 flight to Cairo and that you want on it.

"Please sit. Someone will come."

Nine-fifteen comes before anyone else does. You approach the white shirts again, pointing at your watch. "We want on the 9:15 flight to Cairo."

"Please sit. Someone will come."

The most difficult thing about traveling in Arabic countries is determining which announcement is in English. Several announcements are made, but you are unable to distinguish "Cairo, arrival, departure, Egypt, Jordan, Amman or breakfast" from calls for prayer.

A blue tie comes, well after 9:15. "What is the problem?" he asks. You explain the problem. The others crowd around to listen. They discuss the problem and arrive at a solution. They usher both of you to the security check, and your wife into the metal cabinet. You are frisked by a guard lacking Christian sentiment. He finds something in your left pocket. "What is it?" he asks.

"ChapStick."

"Show it to me." He finds something in your right pocket. "What is it?" he asks.

"Pocketknife," you say, choosing that over "Swiss army knife."

"Trouble," he says. "Show it to me."

You hand him the knife. "That is trouble," he says.

You explain that you carried the knife on safari in Kenya. You show him the scissors for cutting tent cloth, the tweezers for pulling thorns, the toothpick for removing buffalo gristle, the blade for opening bottles of beer, the blade for opening cans of food. You neglect to show him the blade for hijacking airliners.

A white shirt comes over. He and the security guard talk about you. They get into a heated argument. They raise their voices and wave their arms. The white shirt shrugs. "The knife is a problem," he says.

"Give them the knife," your wife shouts from the secure side of the security check. They prevent her from joining your terrorist activities. You explain to the white shirt that you carried the knife through airports in Frankfurt, Nairobi. "It is against the law," the white shirt says. He shows you your ticket. You can't read the Arabic text, but there are drawings of a bomb, a gun, a bullet, a sword, a dagger. You point out that there is no picture of a Swiss knife. He shrugs, passes an upturned palm under your nose and walks away. The gesture is composed equally of contempt and indifference.

"Give them the knife," your wife calls from safety.

It is not that you have an emotional attachment to the knife; you do not want to appear eager to be rid of damning evidence. You suggest that you will not sue the airline if the knife is misplaced.

The security guard, certain that he has found an international terrorist and dreaming of a place in Mecca or wherever security guards go, seizes your camera bag. He takes the camera apart and examines it. He opens every film canister and looks inside. There are twenty-eight of them. He searches your hand luggage. He finds a bottle that looks suspiciously like alcohol. His Islamic soul recoils in horror. "What is it?" he asks. "Mouthwash." He opens the cap. He sniffs the contents. He pours a little into his hand and tastes it. He makes a face. You think he is going to spit.

He finds a canteen. He shakes it. "What is it?" he asks. "Water." He opens the cap. He sniffs the contents. He pours a little in his hand. He tastes it. He makes a face. You think he is going to spit. He barely misses your foot.

"Give him the knife," your wife yells.

The white shirt returns. He explains that he is taking the knife and that it will be put in an envelope and returned to you when you get off the airplane. The security guard is irate. He has caught a terrorist and the white shirts are letting him go. The white shirt tells you to go upstairs and sit down. What about your baggage? You are to go upstairs and sit down, he answers. You have to walk around the security guard. Once again in control of the situation you wink at him with Christian charity.

You join your wife and ride up the escalator that empties into a huge waiting room with ticket stations, duty-free shops and glass walls. None of the ticket stations is open. All are Saudia Airlines. A man is sweeping the floor behind one of them. He has a kind face. If you have a weakness it is that in times of crisis you tend to choose a kind face over a knowledgeable one. "Do you speak English?"

"Yes."

"Has the flight to Cairo left?"

"Yes."

"What time is the next flight to Cairo?"

"Yes."

He knows only one word of English but he listens with such patience and he says "yes" so kindly that you feel better having talked to him. You feel so much better that you approach the next kind face you see. "Do you know if the plane has left for Cairo?"

"Forty-five."

"Forty-five minutes ago or forty-five minutes from now?"

"Forty-five."

You find a door behind one of the ticket counters. You walk inside. Four white shirts turn to stare at your intrusion. They look knowledgeable. Knowledgeable people do not reassure. "Do you speak English?" you ask the most knowledgeable looking.

"A little."

"Can you help me?"

"I doubt it."

You explain your schedule, your itinerary, your commitments. The others crowd in to listen. They talk. They argue. They reach a consensus. You are to go outside and please sit down. Someone will come.

You go outside. You sit. You wait. When your backside turns numb you walk around. You find a white shirt. He has a kind face. Can he help you? "Yes," he says. He takes you to the door you had discovered on your own. Four knowledgeable faces turn to stare. They are not pleased to see you. They do not listen. You are please to be seated. Someone will come.

Someone comes. He brings the same plastic-cased airline breakfast you had eaten on the plane. All you want is coffee, but there is no coffee, so you eat the breakfast instead.

Someone comes. He brings the plastic-cased airline lunch

you would have gotten had you been on the airplane to Amman. Chicken, rice, peas and carrots, juice. You ask for coffee. There is no coffee, so you eat the lunch instead.

Someone comes. You are to go with him and get your bags. Do you need your ticket? No. Do you need your passport? Leave it. You pick up your handbag. Leave it. You take the escalator down and have to pass the security guard. He has not forgotten you. He frisks you in an unfriendly manner.

You are led to the baggage room and asked for your baggage checks. They are on your tickets, upstairs, beyond the security gate. The white shirt looks at the security guard and suggests that you find the bags yourself. You look through three rooms stuffed with baggage to find your own. The baggage clerk wants to check the name on the bags against the name on your passport. Your passport is upstairs, beyond the security gate. The white shirt looks at the security guard, picks up the bags and carries them to customs. The baggage clerk follows behind complaining loudly. The security guard is the only one who listens. The hairs on his Doberman neck bristle. The customs official asks you to unlock the bags. The keys are upstairs, beyond the security gate. The white shirt looks at you. It is a knowledgeable look. "Go get them," he says.

The security guard has been thinking of you. He checks your person in an unofficial manner. You race upstairs, grab your keys and race back to the security gate. The guard has been waiting for you. He checks your person in an unprofessional manner. The customs official unlocks the bags. Everything is removed. The toothbrush container is opened. The toothpaste tube is opened. The dental floss container is opened. Your socks are unrolled. Your shirts are unfolded. Nothing is replaced. You stuff the contents back into the bag, relock it and are told to go upstairs and sit. What about your luggage? Someone will come.

You have to go through security again. Contempt breeds familiarity.

Upstairs, you sit. Someone comes. You are told to pick up your handbags. What about your luggage? Someone will come. You are ushered into a lumbering vehicle that lowers itself to the tarmac, trundles down the taxiway, lifts itself to the airplane cabin door. "Is this the plane to Cairo?" you ask. "Someone will come," the stewardess says.

The airplane takes off. The stewardess comes. She hands you the same airline lunch you have just eaten. Chicken and rice, carrots and peas, juice. This time there is coffee, but you eat the lunch anyway.

You land in Cairo. Inside the terminal you see a white shirt, blue tie and knowledgeable face. "Can you help us?" you ask. "We want the next flight to Amman. We don't care about the route or the airline."

"Sit. Someone will come."

"Should we claim our luggage?"

"Sit. Someone will come."

Two hours later someone comes. He has your luggage. In exchange for your luggage he takes your passports and tickets. You are ushered to a bus. You are driven to a waiting room.

You force your way through a bedlam of passengers who fill every seat, line the walls and sit on the floor. You force your way to a long counter. A verbal fight is taking place between a passenger and two of the clerks. They yell, they gesture, they wave fists in one another's faces. A security guard appears and pushes the passenger away from the counter. The angry clerk turns to you. He is not wearing a white shirt. He is not wearing a blue tie. He has a knowledgeable face. You explain that someone has taken your passports and your tickets to Amman. "Sit until Amman is called," he yells.

There is no place to sit, so you stand close to the counter and study the system. When a plane is about to depart, one of the clerks calls out the destination. "Munich." Passengers bound for Munich fight their way to the counter and passports and tickets are thrown in their general area. The passengers scramble for the passports and tickets, crawl on the floor, wrestle with one another and eventually escape the room.

You do not hear Amman called but you follow some Arabs who push their way to the counter. You push into their midst and say you are going to Amman. You are to sit and wait until Amman is called. The Arabs leave. They return and a clerk begins throwing passports at them. You crowd into their midst. You grab two passports. They are your passports. Inside the passports are tickets. They are your tickets. "I am going to Amman," you yell at the clerk.

"Hurry, they are holding the airplane for you," he yells in return.

"What gate?"

"Ask information."

"Where is information?" He rolls his eyes into his head, shrugs his shoulder and passes an upturned palm beneath your nose. It is a gesture composed equally of contempt and indifference.

You grab your wife and bags and run down the hall until you come to a security guard. "Where is the gate to Amman?"

"Ask information."

"Where is information?"

"Ask the ticket clerks."

A tourist shouts that she has seen a sign saying Amman. You run through the terminal looking for a sign saying Amman. You are waved through a door. You are waved outside the building. You are waved into a waiting bus. "Amman?" you ask the driver. "Forty-five," he says.

The bus stops on the tarmac. You get off. Suitcases stand in curious patterns on the tarmac. You put your bags down. Someone picks them up and adds them to the pattern. Someone else moves them to another part of the pattern. A man comes with a cart and places them on his cart. Another comes and places the bags on his cart. The two men argue. They shout. They gesture. They wrestle over the bags.

You attempt to bring order to the scene. "Amman?" you ask.

Both combatants turn on you. "Get on the airplane," one of them yells. The other gestures, get on the airplane.

"The bags are not tagged," you say, demonstrating where the tag should be. "I do not have a receipt," you say, demonstrating in which pocket you would put the receipt.

"Get on the plane," one of them yells. Get on the plane, the other gestures. You get on the nearest airplane.

"Amman?" you ask the stewardess, who ignores you. No one checks your tickets. The airplane takes off, although it is still fifteen minutes until departure time. The captain comes on the air and in reasonably good English apologizes for the delay in departure. You are on the wrong airplane. Your wife glues herself to a window. You attach yourself to a window on the opposite side of the airplane. You try to determine which direction you are flying. The sun jumps from one wing tip to the other. They are circling to confuse you. You study the ground. Neither of you recalls a large body of water close to Amman.

You find a magazine in the pocket in front of you. *Royal Wings*, published by Royal Jordanian Airlines. Maybe it isn't the right airplane but it's owned by the right country. The "no smoking" sign comes on and preparation is made for landing. You listen closely to the announcement but the only English you hear sounds like "forty-five." You sit while other passengers deplane. You approach the stewardess. "Where are we?" you ask. "Forty-five," she says. "How long will we be here?" "Forty-five." "When will we get to Amman?" "Forty-five."

A few people get aboard and the airplane takes off. You attach yourselves to the window. You study the ground. After a short flight the airplane lands. You wait until the other passengers get off. You approach the stewardess. "Amman?"

"Forty-five," she says.

You get off the airplane. You see a kind face with Christian sentiments. "Do you speak English?" you ask.

"Thank God, Americans. Can you tell me where I catch the next flight to Cairo? We have commitments, itineraries, schedules."

"Where are you now?" you ask.

"Amman."

"Forty-five," you tell him, and pass an upturned palm under his nose. The gesture is composed equally of contempt and indifference. You have arrived.

Women Don't Know

Yeah, ole Doc. Course he wasn't no real doctor or nothing; if he finished high school that was the best he done. Doc was a plumber, and a good one, I bet, although he never talked about it. Martha acted like she was kind of ashamed of it. Women don't admire things like that.

The reason we called him Doc was because him and me was out hunting one time and I saw this nice ten-point buck that run before I could get a shot at it, and he said, "In five minutes that buck's going to put his head in that little clearing right there." Damn if he didn't and I shot him. Good ten-point buck; not a real wide spread but out to his ears and heavy horns.

I said, "How'd you know he was going to do that?" And Doc said, "Smart as I am you ought to call me professor."

And damn if he didn't look like a professor with those thick glasses and that kind of hunched-over look he had like he was examining something real close. I told that story when we got back to camp, but we didn't call him professor — we called him Doc. Everybody but Martha. She called him Harold. Harold, dear. Till the day he died. She couldn't understand how come we called him Doc, and the first time I told her the story how come she looked at me like I told a bad joke. "That was just luck," she said.

Of course it was luck. Doc didn't know what a buck was going to do no more than anybody else, and besides that he couldn't see. Everybody knew it was luck; that's why we called him Doc. If he really knew where a deer was going to poke his head we wouldn't a called him Doc. We'd a called him Elmer Fudd or Barney Fife, the way we called Wilbur Price "Daniel Boone."

"I wish you'd stop calling him Doc," Martha said, when I asked her what she wanted me to do with the horns off that last buck Doc shot. "Now that he's dead it isn't funny anymore." But he'll always be Doc to me. Women don't appreciate things like that.

One time I bought this fake diploma, Doctor of Phunology it said, and hung it in the cabin, and Doc got a bigger kick out of it than anybody. Next time he came out to the lease he was wearing one of them funny flat hats with a tassel like professors wear. Only his was camouflage. If there was one thing ole Doc knew, it was how to have fun. He made fun out of everything. It didn't matter who the fun was on.

Doc was scared of snakes. More than anybody I ever saw. All hunters have a respect for snakes because you're always stepping or sitting where a snake might be, but ole Doc didn't even like pictures of snakes. Well, I got this little rubber snake and put it in his sleeping bag, and when he felt that snake he come out of that bag — tore the zipper off of it. He hit the floor crawling and rolling and skinning his knees, and laughing 'cause he already knew I had tricked him but he still couldn't stop until he was clear on the other side of the cabin. And then he just sat there and laughed. "Damn, they make those things real, don't they?" he said. He got as big a kick out of that as anybody. But he never did get his bag fixed no matter how cold it got. He was afraid I'd do it again.

Doc couldn't see too good, even with those thick glasses on, so he usually hunted with me so I could help him spot deer. I shot this fourteen-pointer one day, horns weren't wide but they had these dog-catchers, and Doc walks up where he can see it and he hauls off and kicks it in the ass. "God damn it, I've been looking for that moose for two years," he said. "Well, get back, I'm going to gut the son of a bitch."

But if a deer moved he'd spot it. I pointed out this real nice twelve-pointer one time but he couldn't see it until the deer ran, and he gut-shot it. Damn, he felt bad about that. We looked for that buck until we found it, but it was dead and the meat wasn't any good. "Well, get the horns and let's go," I told him. It was a wall-hanger but Doc wouldn't take the horns. "You just going to leave them laying there?" I asked him. We were right close to the fence so he gets the idea to wire the deer to the fence so the other hunters would see it standing there and shoot it.

He put it behind some brush where you didn't get a real good view of it and propped its head up so it was looking at you and you could see those horns. Nice heavy horns. One of the best bucks I ever saw on this lease. We drove off aways and stopped to see how it looked, and damn if it didn't look good. I started to drive off, and Doc says, "Wait a minute, that looks so good I'm going to shoot it myself," and he did, right in the neck where he should have shot it the first time. I think everybody on the lease shot at that deer until somebody finally took the horns.

Ole Doc felt bad about me having to spot for him, so he devised this plan to help me out. I had spotted this real nice buck in Buck Valley but I never could get a shot at it, so Doc told me to climb up over the Turkey Tracks and down into the valley, and him and Wilbur Price were going to drive the long way around the road, and they was going to walk in and run that deer out the other end of the valley right by where I was going to be sitting. Wilbur was the sorriest hunter I ever saw. There was a little milk-sucker that we saw every time we left the cabin that nobody else would even shoot at and Wilbur missed it twice.

I got up three hours before daylight and took my flashlight — and oh, it was cold. And rough. I was having to climb over those three hills with a flashlight in one hand and rifle in the other and before I got to the second one my flashlight burned out. I stumbled over rocks and cactus and ran into mesquite and catclaw, and I was all tore up by the time I got to Buck Valley. And sweaty. And 'course the minute I sat down my sweat got cold.

But I got there in time to let everything get quiet around me so the deer would forget I was there, and along about daylight I hear Doc's truck rattling down the road. I'm shivering so I don't know if I can hit anything, but they're coming down the road, so I get ready as best I can. Then I hear this shot, and I hear the truck doors slam, and I can hear them talking. After a while the doors slam, the truck starts and they drive away, and I'm yelling, "Doc, Doc, wait for me."

They drive off and leave me. I sit there for a while getting colder and colder and trying to think what to do. Walk a hell of a way around the road or climb back over those three hills. I go back over the hills. I walk into camp and there is Wilbur skinning my deer. And it's better than I thought it was. It's Boone and Crockett. It looks like a damn moose.

I walk into the cabin and there is Doc having lunch. "Hey, did you see that big buck Wilbur killed?" Doc says. I am so mad I can't even speak. Then it dawns on Doc what he did. "You climbed over the Turkey Tracks."

"Twice," I remind him.

"Sit down, I'm going to fix you a sandwich."

"To hell with it. You'd probably forget to put the bread on it," I tell him.

Ole Doc is trying hard not to laugh but I can see his shoulders shaking. "How in the hell did you and Wilbur ever kill a deer?" I asked him. "You can't see and he can't shoot."

"Damn buck was chasing a doe," he said, "and stopped right in front of the truck to look at us, and Wilbur shot it. I got so excited about him finally getting a buck that I just forgot." He just had to laugh then, and I couldn't help it, I laughed too.

"I bet that's the only buck Wilbur ever shoots," I say, and damn if I'm not right. The next day Wilbur comes in, starts unloading his rifle and fires a shot through the cabin. There are three hunters in the cabin and he's such a sorry shot he misses all of them, but the other hunters vote not to ask him back. They don't want him on the lease.

I paid ole Doc back, although I didn't mean to. One year there was this wild hog that kept tearing up fences and getting into the oat fields, so the rancher hired a man to come in with dogs and kill it. The boar killed two dogs and put the dog man up a tree. Oh, it was mean. So the rancher hired another man with dogs and asked us hunters if we'd help. Everybody wanted to kill that boar, but I knew Doc didn't have a chance because it would be at night and he wouldn't be able to see it.

So I devised a plan. I see where this hog leaves the oat field and goes down this draw, and the draw gets deep and narrow at this one point so that if the hog's in there, that's where he's got to stay. So me and Doc dig a hole in that narrow place, and Doc lays down in it, and I tell him, "When that boar hears those dogs he's going to come right through here and he's going to be close enough so you can see him, but for God's sake don't miss." That damn hog was a killer.

Well, Doc lays down, and he waits and he waits. And he has a couple of drinks to stay warm, and he goes to sleep. All of a sudden he hears this racket and looks up and there is this big boar coming right at him. He doesn't even have time to raise his rifle. He just covered his head with his arms and the boar ran down his back and broke two ribs. Ole Doc couldn't laugh because he hurt so, but he said it wasn't the boar running down his back that hurt so much — it was the dogs jumping on his broke ribs.

I took him to the hospital and called Martha, and by the time she got there they knew he didn't have no internal injuries, and when I told her about ole Doc laying there and the hog running down his back I couldn't keep from laughing. But there was no laughter in that woman. Women don't think things like that are funny.

After that she kind of blamed me for everything. But I couldn't stop him from hunting any more than she could. Doc wasn't supposed to drink and he didn't bring anything to the lease, but somebody always had a bottle and he'd usually join in. But nobody drank much anymore. Not like the old days. One time back then Doc ran into town and bought a whole case of champagne.

"What are we celebrating?" we asked. We thought Doc must have shot the moose he was always talking about.

"My turkey," he said. Doc had seen this turkey and shot it and when he went over to pick it up, it was an owl that had caught a mouse. Doc saw that mouse hanging down from the owl's beak and thought it was a turkey beard. We laughed and got drunk and puked all over the cabin. God, it was a mess.

Ole Doc laughed more than anybody about that. Course we didn't tell the rancher, because he would have raised hell about shooting an owl. So would the game warden. We didn't tell Martha either. Women don't understand things like that.

We don't drink like that anymore. Too old, I guess. I told Martha that. She said, "All I know is, if he'd stayed home he'd be alive now."

Maybe he would have. Maybe he'd a been alive and wished he wasn't. I don't know that either, but I do know he died doing what he liked best. He was up in the Turkey Tracks and shot a buck and was trying to drag it out by himself. He should have come back and got one of us to help him, but he was proud of himself and he wanted to bring that buck back to camp and show us what he'd done. He'd finally got that moose he was always talking about.

When he didn't come in for lunch we got worried about him and went looking. It was late in the evening when we found him. He was just sitting there, leaned back against that buck like he was waiting for us to find him, waiting for us to see what he had done. He had kind of a smile on his face and he would a been looking at us if the birds hadn't gotten to him first. Damn birds.

Sometimes I wish I'd a been with him when he shot that buck. I'd a helped him drag it out and he'd still be alive. Then I think, Doc didn't want no help. That's why he went off by himself. He wanted to find that deer and shoot it and show it all by himself. I didn't tell Martha that. I didn't tell her about the birds either. That's the first thing a man would'a asked, but women don't want to know things like that, so I didn't tell her. I just told her he was sitting there with the biggest deer he'd ever shot. I didn't mention his eyes at all.

The paper did a story on him, and Martha told how he had his own plumbing company and the clubs and church he belonged to and how he had been president of the Chamber of Commerce and member of the City Council. That didn't surprise me none, but we didn't talk about things like that. Course I knew he had been in the war — we talked about that and where all we'd been — but I didn't know that he got a medal for putting out a chemical fire and that was why his eyes were so bad. You don't tell friends things like that and ole Doc and me was friends although I only saw him at the hunting lease.

I packed up his gear the way he would have wanted me to and took it to Martha. She took his rifle for her son and she said, "There's two things you can do for me. Stop calling him Doc and burn those old clothes." Course Doc did wear old clothes a wino wouldn't die in, especially that old Navy coat that probably went through the fire with him, but I guess I looked at her kind of funny. "Harold wasn't like that," Martha said. "He was a very successful man. You didn't really know him."

Martha told the paper that he had died hunting, the way he wanted to, which I thought was nice of her to say. She didn't mention his first wife at all, which I thought she should have, Mary being dead and all. And I was surprised that he had a stepson. I don't remember him ever mentioning that.

Martha didn't tell them the most important thing of all. She didn't tell them how good a buck he got. Women don't understand things like that.

At Play in the Sewers of the Lord

Thurgood had been all night on his knees praying for deliverance from a sewer. It was not an entirely unfamiliar position for him, but it was an unfamiliar subject. Perhaps priests blessed sewers, perhaps television evangelists prayed for profits, but he had not. Not before now. Other godly men prayed for deliverance from temptation, from persecution, from ecclesiastical authority and congregational prejudice. Thurgood prayed that God would deliver him from a sewage plant.

He had prayed more over the sewage plant than over the happiness of his marriage, the education of his children, the debt of his church, the splinter group that was angry about the book that was used in the children's Sunday School or the three women who sat on the back pew and talked throughout the service. And it was all his father's fault.

His father had always wanted him to be a partner in the family business — the sewage business — and had never been happy that his only son had become a minister. It wasn't the sewage business Thurgood disliked so much, it was all business; all that grubby concern over prices, and buying and selling. He had wanted his life to deal with something better than that. "I want to do something important," he had explained to his father.

"Get in that methane gas and you'll find out what's important," his father said.

"I want people to look up to me."

"Shut down the sewage plant for a day or two and they'll look up to you," his father said. "Shut it down for a week and they'll think you're God." His father understood sewage and believed that made him an expert on religion.

Thurgood thought he had fled that life forever, but his dying father had bequeathed him the sewage plant, making him not a partner but sole proprietor. At first he had not been ungrateful. It was a small, independent business that treated sewage from unincorporated housing areas, mostly mobile homes and house trailers. His father had done well enough that his mother could aspire to unexceptional social clubs and that Thurgood could attend unremarkable colleges and seminaries. Well enough that when his mother had died, his father had made him a settlement that had given Thurgood a measure of independence and had permitted him to hold liberal, even socialistic, views.

Since Thurgood lived in another state, after his father's funeral he had asked R. B. Abernathy, the oldest and most trusted of his father's employees, to run the business. R. B. was an alcoholic who went with the property. He kept the books and was responsible for chlorination, pH balance and suspended particles. R. B. was reliable with anything that was not distilled. The only other employee was Elroy, who had been there less than three months. Elroy, who had aspired to a military career but had three times failed the I.Q. tests, was in charge of sludge. The sewage business did not attract the career-minded.

Thurgood had washed his hands of the matter, returning to his church and to matters of the spirit. Within days, R. B. informed him that his father, during his final illness, had let business slide. The equipment was still being paid for and the past year the business had lost money. His father's savings had been wiped out.

The matter was troubling but not yet dispiriting. Thurgood had directed R. B. to sell the business and had made up the monthly deficit out of the inheritance from his mother. But small, independent sewage plants were not hot properties. After some months there had been only one offer, that from a large firm that offered to buy the water pumps, air pumps and clarifying tanks, leaving his father's employees jobless and his father's customers sewer-less. Thurgood had on principle rejected the offer.

Then a longtime prayer was answered. He returned to his hometown as pastor of the church in which he had been reared. Why were the wrong prayers always answered? Why were they answered in an untimely fashion? He had dreamed of returning to the town as a saintly and successful son; he had returned as the owner of a troubled sewage plant. What sin had he committed that this punishment should be visited upon him? He was rapidly becoming one of the middle-class poor and his only hope for financial salvation was to betray his father's employees and customers by selling the equipment, or to take the course R. B. advised and raise the sewer rates.

He had raised the rates. Jesus had caused less consternation raising Lazarus. Letters, some from his parishioners, were written to the newspapers calling him a money-sucking "propheteer" who sold his soul for a few bucks. Elroy wanted to firebomb the letter writers using R. B.'s cache of empty bottles for bombs. Instead, Thurgood had, despite his wife's advice, written to the paper detailing his financial situation, believing that if people knew they would understand. He had been in error.

Most of the slanderers paid the new rate, but a certain Helga Kierchoff continued to pay the rate she had always paid. Thurgood had, despite his wife's advice, gone to the woman personally to explain that under the old rates he lost money every month. He thought if he explained the situation to her she would be fair. He had been in error.

Helga Kierchoff had been left a few acres of land by her father, and she leased it to thirty-six families who lived in house trailers. Thirty-six families depended upon his sewage plant and Helga's protection, and Helga, who saw the land as fiefdom and herself as lord, declared in a vulgar and offensive manner that she was not going to pay the new rates while seventy-two vassals cheered and their children learned a new and impressive vocabulary.

Thurgood went home and, without reporting the matter to his wife or R. B., ignored Helga and her families until R. B. insisted that he was going to have to require the new rate or declare bankruptcy. Thurgood went to a lawyer who advised bankruptcy as it was the more complicated and would require the lawyer's services for the longer time. At Thurgood's insistence, the attorney informed him that he had the right, after notification, to cut the sewer line. The attorney agreed, for a fee, to write a letter informing Helga Kierchoff of this fact. "She'll weep when she reads this," the lawyer chortled. "You got her by the short hairs now." Miss Kierchoff returned the letter to Thurgood with marks that suggested proximity to the short hairs.

Thurgood considered giving the sewage plant to the church. The church could find a buyer, raise the rates, declare bankruptcy or deprive thirty-six families of sewer service. Maybe, if the plant sold right away, there would be some money for charity. God could do that. Maybe if it was the church's burden, God would have to come in and save the church from scandal. It appeared that God wasn't going to save him. Thurgood discussed the matter with the church leaders, who declined the gift.

With much prayer and supplication that he not lose his temper, that he not lose his courage, and that he not lose his life, he went again to explain the situation to Miss Kierchoff. Miss Kierchoff, whom God had created to make Golda Meir look glamorous and the Ayatollah Khomeini seem reasonable, steadfastly refused to understand his position, leaving Thurgood no choice but to declare his intention to cut the sewer line. Miss Kierchoff hoped he drowned in effluent.

He returned home determined to give Miss Kierchoff no more than three weeks of grace. He found his wife in the living room listening to the television news. Miss Kierchoff, a poor, humble, disadvantaged Christian lady, described to the television cameras how thirty-six families, including veterans, were being denied sewer service by a greedy, hypocritical draft dodger and child abuser. "Taking a potty from a child is child abuse," Helga shouted. In the background fathers made menacing gestures, mothers wept and children wailed for the camera. How could God have put such power in the hands of his enemy? Thurgood's wife, who had never cared for religious controversy, took to her bed.

He had waited three weeks, even four, praying that God would lead the benighted woman to her senses or strike her dead. God refused. In the meantime, Thurgood was unable to meet the payroll. R. B. wept over the books in every bar in town, begging his cronies to find an uncounted dollar. Elroy threatened to torch the sewage plant if he was laid off. Thurgood promised them a showdown with Helga Kierchoff.

After a night on his knees in prayer — "Why me, O Lord?" — he faced the prospect of television cameras, newspaper reporters and Helga Kierchoff with the flag, the cross and thirty-six families wrapped around her, turning even the dogs against him. She was going to look like Mother Teresa;

he was going to look like Scrooge, bringing scandal to his wife, his children and the church he wanted to honor.

That he should come to this: a faithful if demanding husband, a kind if boring father, a pleasant if pedantic minister. If not righteous, at least not self-righteous. He had never even gotten a parking ticket. That would all change today because God, the God of mercy and of love, had refused, despite his fervent prayer, to deliver him from Helga Kierchoff. He had never questioned the Lord before. At least not so vehemently.

Outside, Elroy honked the truck's horn, signaling that it was time to go. Reluctantly, Thurgood abandoned his prayers. If God would not save him, he would have to save himself. He would, on television, blame everything on R. B. and publicly fire him. No, that was unworthy. And would probably bring a lawsuit. He would blame everything on Elroy. Elroy would torch him in his sleep. He would put the business in his wife's name. Too late for that. He would donate the sewage plant to the Salvation Army, the Pope, a television evangelist —

Elroy honked again. "We gonna kick ass today," Elroy shouted. Thurgood invited his wife to go with him to the trailer park but that devout woman, who was never devious except early in the morning — "I'm awake, I'm up" — professed to have an allergy to bright lights. Thurgood walked outside and saw R. B. and Elroy waiting in the truck, Elroy holding a shotgun between his knees. He persuaded Elroy to let him carry the shotgun, locked it in the trunk of his car, and led them into battle. In the rearview mirror he saw Elroy put on his hardhat and R. B. fortify himself with strong spirit.

The termagant was waiting for him wearing a white robe and clutching a Bible in her hands. Wailing babies clung to her feet. Fathers and mothers chanted "free sewer, free sewer," and waved banners that read "Children Before Profits," "Sewage Is An Inalienable Right" and "Veterans Against Slit Trenches." While Thurgood stared at Helga, amazed at the lengths she would go to protect her customers, Elroy jumped out of the truck and began uncovering the sewer line. Cautiously Thurgood approached Helga, clinging to the strength of his prayers. "I come in peace," he said, holding up a hand, aware that on television he was going to look like a Pilgrim greeting an Indian before robbing him.

"How?" she said.

"If you would just look at the books," he said, gesturing at R. B., who was leafing through the books as though looking for dollar bills between the pages.

"We're ready to cut her," Elroy yelled, posing over the concrete sewer line, holding the air hammer like a machine gun.

"Not yet," Thurgood said.

Reluctantly Elroy relaxed his pose. "Just following orders," Elroy obliged the cameras. "If the man says 'cut the sewer' I cut the sewer."

Thurgood took the books from R. B. and offered them to the cameras. "If I could just break even," he said.

"Who keeps these books?" Helga demanded.

Thurgood looked at R. B., who sat on the step side of the truck singing softly to himself. "R. B. is my business manager."

"You want me to accept books kept by a drunk?"

"I'm willing to compromise," Thurgood said, trying to drown out R. B., who had the attention of the cameras.

"No compromise," the crowd shouted. "No compromise."

"Deadbeats don't deserve sympathy," Elroy said. "Like the reverend says, 'if they got to go, they got to pay.'"

"No pay," shouted thirty-six families. "No pay."

Thurgood devoutly wished he could give Elroy to Miss Kierchoff. They deserved each other.

"As God is my witness," Helga said, spreading her arms and looking dramatically into the heavens, "I will not compromise the health and well-being of thirty-six families. Here I stand." She spread her legs as wide as her arms and held the pose.

"If you would just give us a little space," Thurgood said to the cameramen, "I think we could work out something."

"No compromise, no compromise," shouted thirty-six families.

"Your thirty-six families are driving me into bankruptcy," Thurgood said. "They are depriving my employees —" he waved an arm at his employees and the camera followed the gesture, capturing R. B. sucking at his bottle and Elroy demonstrating how he was going to cut the sewer line.

"You'll cut my head off before you cut off my families," Helga screamed, lying over the exposed sewer line, offering Elroy her neck.

Thurgood imposed his body in front of Helga before Elroy could demonstrate how he would sever her head. Despite his anger, Thurgood had a grudging admiration for her. She was loyal to her customers, and in their defense she was a formidable opponent. "If we could confine our discussion to economics —" Thurgood suggested.

"It's not a question of economics," said Helga, holding her prone position for the cameras. "It's a question of management."

Ignoring the cameras Thurgood raised his eyes to heaven. It was impossible to reason with such a woman. If God refused a thunderbolt, he was lost. Why couldn't God give — into Thurgood's tortured brain crept a revelation more powerful than a thunderbolt. It was more blessed to give than to receive.

"Do you think you could do a better job of managing the sewage plant?" Thurgood asked hopefully.

"I know I could do a better job," Helga said.

Another revelation: pride preceded fall. "And could you do that without depriving these men of their jobs?" Thurgood asked, unwillingly focusing the cameras on R. B., who was searching under the truck seat for another bottle, and on Elroy, who had put down the air hammer and was entertaining the children by balancing the hardhat upside down on his head.

Helga was sitting up now, having lost both her certainty and her pose. It was too late; Thurgood had the attention of the cameras. Whatsoever thy hand findeth to do, do quickly. He picked up the discarded air hammer, hoping the grunt wasn't audible on television. "I give you the sewage plant," he said, placing the air hammer across her lap and pinning her to the ground.

Thurgood held out his arms to the cameras. "I give the sewage plant and all property and rights thereof to Helga Kierchoff. Free, I give it. Without charge. With only one condition. That these faithful employees be allowed to keep their jobs for as long as they wish."

"Free sewer," the families shouted, "free sewer."

Helga had struggled out from under the air hammer and approached him waving a finger, but before she could speak he grabbed her hand and shook it in both of his. "Agreed," he said. Let her lawyers get out of that without R. B. filing a lawsuit and Elroy torching the plant. "It's done. It's all yours."

Meekly Thurgood turned from the reporters, who were gushing "magnanimous gesture" into their microphones. Humbly he bestowed upon Helga a sewage plant, two faithful employees and the attention of the media. While Helga stumbled from saint to martyr, from victim to victor trying to strike the right pose, Thurgood slipped away, the glow of Christian charity radiant in his smile.

Things No One Told Me

When Miss Codd died, I went home for her funeral. Sidney Slocum wasn't there — the state had taken him when his folks got old — but almost everyone in the county was. Good teachers are remembered after they're gone. That was one of the things no one told me but that I learned anyway.

When I was in second grade I believed Miss Codd had read every book ever written and had to start over. "And she's still not smart enough to teach Sidney Slocum how to write his own name," I told my classmates. I had no idea how many books had been written, but I was certain Miss Codd had read them, and I believed that if she couldn't teach Sidney Slocum anything, I couldn't.

Sidney and I were in third grade when he became my

problem. As far as I could tell, Sidney had always been in the third grade and always would be. Sidney was at least six feet tall and old enough to be in high school, maybe college. Everyone thought Miss Codd should have graduated Sidney to get rid of him. We thought she was trying to save him by teaching him to read and write. Miss Codd thought she could save everybody.

Mothers whispered that Sidney was "slow" and "wasn't right." We were afraid of him, called him stupid behind his back and played tricks on him when we thought we could get away with it. Miss Codd wouldn't permit us to be mean to Sidney, and he had a fierce temper. That was half the fun, teasing Sidney until he got angry and then running and screaming until Miss Codd saved us.

Being chased around the playground by Sidney was like being chased by Frankenstein. Sidney had the same awkward, shuffling gait, the same broad, uncomprehending face and a mouth that wasn't big enough for all his teeth. "Get-get-get you," he'd pant. When angry, Sidney was the terror of the school and only Miss Codd stood between us and him.

Miss Codd, who had seemed ancient but was probably in her fifties, was small, shapeless as a teddy bear, and a strict disciplinarian. Sidney was as afraid of her as we were of the two of them together. She made no exceptions. When Sidney misbehaved she paddled him although he was twice her size.

When she caught him peeking in the girls' two-hole privy, Sidney ran away from school rather than take his licking. Miss Codd left the school in charge of one of the older girls, Emily Turvaville, and went after Sidney. Some of the boys threw erasers and spit wads while Emily threatened to take their names, but I prayed that Miss Codd never find Sidney and that he never come back to school. Miss Codd found him hiding in a cotton patch and led him back by the ear, although he had to bend over for her to reach it.

Mine was one of the fortunate families. We lived on our own land and had cows, pigs, chickens and a garden. We didn't go hungry. Sidney's folks were sharecroppers on a weedy place that wasn't fit for crops or kids. After Sidney was born his parents gave up on kids. That's what folks said.

There were three of us in third grade, four counting Sidney, who didn't belong. I had kept my distance from Sidney until third grade, and I didn't want him in my class. There wasn't a desk in school big enough for him. When we were called to the front of the room for recitation, Sidney sprawled out of his desk and into my space. Not daring to kick his foot, which was under my desk, like I would have done with another third grader, I asked him to move it. Sidney didn't hear or didn't heed.

"Would you move your clodhopper?" I said a little louder. Miss Codd gave me a stern, disapproving look, but the titter of laughter I got from my classmates compensated for it. When I turned around, I saw everyone was looking at me. I was the center of attention. All I had to do to be noticed was to tease dumb Sidney and outsmart Miss Codd, who thought she could save him. It was one of those things no one told me but that I learned anyway.

I became Sidney's chief tormentor. I hid Sidney's pencil, the only one he had, when he wasn't looking. I switched my short pencil for his longer one. I turned his book upside down so that Miss Codd had to tell him to turn it back. Once, while Miss Codd was writing on the blackboard, I tied his shoelace to my desk so that when we were dismissed, he fell in the aisle, toppling desks and scattering books.

Miss Codd never caught me at it — his rotten shoelace broke — but she suspected I was guilty. She talked to me about what she called "gifts" and told me to be kind to Sidney. I kept my fingers crossed when I promised I would and the first chance I got, hid his lunch. His lunch was always the same, a couple of stale biscuits in a syrup bucket that had holes punched in the top so that the biscuits didn't sweat.

A lot of kids used syrup buckets as lunch pails and put them on a shelf in the cloakroom. Sidney could never remember where he put his lunch so Miss Codd had Sidney print his name on his bucket with fingernail polish. It was one of her failed attempts to teach Sidney to write his name and the bucket had indecipherable nail polish on one side.

Hiding the bucket was a matter of turning it so the polish didn't show. Sidney wailed and slobbered looking for his pail and I basked in the knowing looks I got from the other children who watched to see if I got away with it. I told Miss Codd he must have turned his bucket the wrong way, the way he turned his book upside down and didn't know it. The other children giggled. I was not only funny, I was daring. I enjoyed their laughter so much that I later put my sandwich in my coat pocket, filled my bucket with water and set it upside down on top of Sidney's lunch so that the water leaked from my bucket into his.

Sidney's biscuits had disintegrated by lunch time and, unable to get them out with his hands, Sidney turned up the bucket and drank his lunch. I laughed and some of the older boys laughed with me. Some of the kids felt sorry for Sidney. One of the girls gave Sidney part of her sandwich. Miss Codd reminded us that Sidney was larger than we were and needed more food. She didn't say that Sidney never had enough to eat but warned us that if anyone ruined Sidney's lunch again the whole school would go without lunch to see how it felt.

On the playground some of the girls told me I was mean and the other boys didn't take up for me the way they usually sided boys against the girls. For any boy except Sidney. I learned my lesson. I could tease Sidney, I could show how awkward and stupid he was, but I couldn't make him look pitiful and I couldn't bring punishment on the other children and be popular.

I sulked for a couple of days and ignored Sidney. When that didn't work, I joined in the playground games but Jervis could swing higher and jump farther from the single swing we had than anyone in school. Garland brought to school an owl's foot that had strings attached to the tendons so that he could walk up behind unsuspecting girls and pinch them on the arm with it. All the boys wanted to see the foot and all the girls wanted him to chase them with it.

Then one day, Sidney hit the ball instead of slinging the bat into the outfield. When they chose up sides to play ball, I was usually near the last but Sidney was always chosen last. Even after the girls. He couldn't hit the ball, he couldn't catch the ball, he couldn't throw it and he couldn't run. Then one day he hit the ball all the way to the ditch. It took three throws to get it home and if Sidney hadn't been so slow and missed a base or two, it would have been a home run.

Everyone crowded around, laughing at how far Sidney hit the ball, and how he had failed to tag all the bases and had run back to first base when he saw Jervis had the ball at home. Sidney wasn't exactly the hero, but he thought he was. He grinned and laughed with all his teeth spilling out of his mouth. "Hit-hit-hit it," he said like he had a hard time talking around all his teeth. "Hit it to the — to the ditch."

The boys laughed and clapped Sidney on the shoulders. The girls watched the boys and giggled behind their hands. I was ignored. The kids were drifting away when I started yelling. "Hey, Sidney. Sidney. You hit the ball so far you're going to be promoted to fourth grade." They stopped to watch.

Sidney had been in third grade so long it took him a while to comprehend fourth grade. "You're going to be promoted, Sidney," I said. "All you have to do is spell P.T.A. Can you spell P.T.A.?"

The other kids watched Sidney and grinned. "P.T.A.," I said. "Can you spell P.T.A.?"

Sidney was scared. Everyone had watched him hit the ball and run the bases. They had crowded around and laughed but no one had teased or pointed at him the way they usually did. Now, that was about to change, and it was almost painful watching him try to think.

"Come on, Sidney, you can be in fourth grade," I taunted. Sidney looked at the smiling faces around him but found no help. "I'll help you out, Sidney," I said. "The first letter is P."

"P," Sidney said, more in bewilderment than gratitude.

"The second letter is P."

"P.P.," Sidney said.

The boys laughed and pointed, the girls ran off screaming and I was basking in glory when Sidney realized I had made fun of him. I thought he was going to cry, then he grabbed me by the throat, lifting me off the ground. The sky was turning dark and the ground was spinning when Miss Codd appeared and made Sidney put me down. She made him sit in a corner the rest of the day and kept me after school until she was sure I could swallow and that he had gone home. Sidney couldn't remember individual cruelties from one class period to the next, much less over the weekend.

When Miss Codd asked what had happened on the playground, I said I was trying to teach Sidney to spell P.T.A. I still thought it was funny and bit my lip to keep from laughing.

Miss Codd said she was pleased I wanted to help Sidney and for the rest of the year I would stay in during lunch and recess and help Sidney with his lessons. I almost cried at that. It was a month until the end of school and the other boys would be out on the playground getting attention by popping the heads off snakes, setting ants on fire with matches they had sneaked from home and peeling scabs from their elbows and knees.

I hoped Miss Codd would relent or forget but Monday she reminded me when I started outside at recess. The first day I tried to teach Sidney to spell his name, something Miss Codd had never taught him. Failing at that, I tried to teach him numbers from one to ten, from one to five, one to three. Just as I thought, I couldn't teach him anything.

Day after day I was stuck with Sidney while the other children played. In desperation, I did Sidney's lessons for him. It didn't work. No matter how poorly I made the letters and numbers, Miss Codd recognized my work and gave it back to me. Sidney wasn't afraid of me like he was Miss Codd. I couldn't make him work, I couldn't stop him from eating my lunch and I couldn't keep him from sprawling all over his desk and mine.

"Why can't you sit straight?" I asked him.

"It-it-it feels like I'm-I'm-I'm crooked," he said.

"I'm sorry," I told Miss Codd, believing "sorry" was the answer to everything. "I'll never mistreat him again," I said, believing good intentions covered everything that sorry didn't.

Miss Codd did not relent. "You're making me hate him," I said. She had read every book there was to read and it hadn't helped her teach him. "How long do I have to help him?"

"Until the lesson is learned," she said. That's how I knew she kept Sidney in school because she could not admit failure. She had to prove she could teach anyone.

"But he's not learning anything," I said.

"Everyone can learn if they have the right teacher," she said. I thought I would be saddled with Sidney until he married or I got to high school.

I didn't know where to begin teaching Sidney, and, after a couple of weeks of trying to explain how to do his lessons, I gave up. Sometimes we drew on the blackboard. I drew and he marked. Mostly, we sat together, his foot under my desk and his elbow on it, staring at a book or the floor or the wall, listening to the squeals and laughter of the children on the playground.

That summer I hoped that Sidney would die or that his folks would move or that he wouldn't come back to school, but on the first day there he was. Again, I tried to slip outside at recess, hoping Miss Codd had forgotten. She hadn't. "How long do I have to do this?" I cried. "I hate school."

"Until the lesson is learned," she said.

By the end of the first recess, I knew Sidney had not gotten any smarter over the summer and that I was going to spend the whole year without getting to show off on the playground. Not only that, Sidney had been promoted and I had to sit beside him with his foot under my desk and his arm on the back of my chair during recitation. The other kids laughed at me as much as at him.

We stared at the books and floor some more and drew on the blackboard. I made circles and he drew Xs through them. He liked that. He still ate my lunch or whatever he got before I got to it. One day he showed me a fishing lure. It was painted like a minnow. The hook had rusted off and most of the paint was gone. I looked at it and gave it back. "It's useless, Sidney. You know what useless means? It's like you're dead."

"Dead lose their-their spit," he said, losing his all over my desk.

He was right in a way, but then it was all wrong too. "Why do you come to school, Sidney? You don't learn anything. You don't have any friends."

"I," he said, his voice trailing off into nothing. "I learn you."

"You know me," I corrected. "But you don't, Sidney. You can't learn anything."

I was wrong. Sidney learned to play tic-tac-toe. Rather, he learned to make Xs in the squares I had marked on the blackboard. He didn't understand what winning meant; at least, he didn't mind when he lost. I let him win sometimes, but it was playing that he enjoyed. Miss Codd caught us at it once. She didn't say anything but Sidney sat down at his desk and whimpered and I couldn't get him to play again until the next day.

The other kids had forgotten how smart I had been and started calling me dummy and saying Sidney and I had to stay in because we were stupid. I thought of siccing Sidney on them; I thought I could do it, but I didn't. I tried to show how smart I was during recitation and spelling bees. They didn't call me dumb as much after that but they asked why I didn't play with them, why I spent all my time with Sidney.

"I have to help him with his lessons," I said one morning before school, hoping to convince them I was smart.

"That dummy? He can't learn anything."

"He can play tic-tac-toe," I said. "I taught him." To prove it, I drew some lines on the playground and Sidney made an X. We didn't get to play, though, because Miss Codd came outside and rang the bell for us to line up before we marched inside.

After lunch, Miss Codd told Sidney and me we could go outside. "I taught him to play tic-tac-toe," I said. She smiled the tight smile she used when we had learned our lessons.

Sidney and I were the last ones chosen for softball; we both struck out and the third baseman had to duck when Sidney lost the bat. When our side took the field, we were sent out near the ditch with the little kids who couldn't catch or throw. That made me mad. I sat on the ground and sulked. Sidney came and sat beside me. Even outside he sprawled in my space. He took a stick and drew lines on the ground, wanting to play tic-tac-toe. I did, but I didn't let him win because some of the little kids had come over to watch. "I taught him," I told them.

At the end of the year, Sidney was sent back to third grade. I moved on to fifth, sixth, seventh. Sidney was never promoted again, and I never looked back.

I didn't think about Sidney again until I came home for Miss Codd's funeral and he wasn't there. Good teachers are remembered after they're gone.

The Perfect Gift

Gifts were tests. At least to Christians. Maxwell was convinced of that. And he had never passed the test. Maxwell had never forgotten an anniversary, birthday or Christmas, but neither had he ever gotten Beth a perfect gift, a present that matched the gifts she had given him, a present that pleased her as much as the gifts her friend Shirley gave her. And Shirley hadn't even gone to college. Shirley had wasted her life running a frame shop. Shirley had been married four times.

Beth said that she liked his presents. She thanked him and kissed him, but when she didn't call him her "wise man bearing gifts," he knew he had failed again.

This time was going to be different. He was in his third year of teaching philosophy at the local community college, he no longer had to read the prices first on the menu in the faculty lounge and for his fifth wedding anniversary he was going to surprise, delight, amaze and confound his wife with the perfect gift.

It wasn't that Beth was hard to please. She was delighted with everything he gave her, although she said the diamond wedding set, which he had borrowed money to buy, was too expensive and she was happy just to be his wife. Sometimes, Beth was too easy to please. Like the art history class where the only thing she studied was slides, the church she and Shirley attended that didn't have entrance exams or a Ph.D. for a pastor, the brass umbrella stand Shirley had given them for a wedding present.

"We don't even have an umbrella," he said.

"We'll put it in the hall," Beth said.

"We don't have a hall," he reminded her.

Beth put it beside the bed and kept dried flowers in it.

Rather than studying philosophy, Beth had majored in art history. Instead of going to graduate school, she had worked in Shirley's frame shop. If she hadn't, they wouldn't have been able to get married, but sometimes he thought she would understand him better if she too had gone to graduate school, had studied philosophy, if she read J. S. Mill instead of T. S. Eliot, Plato instead of St. Paul. Nevertheless, he loved her simplicity and her naiveté and tried to reward it.

For their first anniversary he had given her a gold chain. Beth said that she liked having nice things but that the chain was too expensive. It was expensive, considering Beth's salary, but gold was a better value than the ceramic butterfly Shirley had given her.

"Ceramic is worthless once you take it out of the store," he explained. "Or if you break it," he said when a wing came off.

"I'll use it for a paperweight," Beth said. "And the wing can be a bookmark."

Maxwell was a fast learner. Beth did not want expensive or impractical gifts, so for Christmas he gave her a microwave. Shirley gave her scented candles. For her birthday he gave her a hand vacuum. Shirley gave her a plastic cigarette lighter with bits of gaudy colored glass stuck to it.

"You don't even smoke," he snorted.

"I'll use it to light the candles," she said.

"A box of matches would have been more utilitarian, more economical and more attractive," he pointed out. He was getting his Ph.D. in philosophy. He knew better than Shirley what was good and beautiful.

For her birthday he gave Beth membership in a health club because he thought the exercise would relax her after being at work all day, and he needed solitude to work on his dissertation. For their anniversary, he gave her a subscription to a sophisticated magazine likely to improve her mind. Shirley took them to an expensive restaurant for dinner, complete with wine and singing waiters.

"I thought Shirley knew you better than that," Maxwell smirked when they were alone.

"This is an evening I'll never forget," Beth said.

Maxwell knew his wife too well to think she cared for luxury or the gratification of temporal appetites. It was the experience she liked, so for Christmas he took her to Las Vegas for two days. Shirley gave her a glass angel as a Christmas tree ornament. "It's such a shameless little angel," Beth said, adoring it. And Maxwell knew. When it was too late to cancel the reservations, Maxwell knew once again he had failed the test.

When Maxwell accepted a job at the small community college in another state, Beth had said good-bye to her job and Shirley, although Shirley always remembered their anniversary. Beth had been unable to find a job in the small town or an older confidante like Shirley. The older faculty wives were arrogant because of their husbands' rank and tenure. The younger faculty wives were fearful that she might find favor with the dean's wife, whose approval was more important than publication. Beth wasn't entirely happy in their new home and Maxwell was going to make up for it with the perfect, well-chosen gift.

Maxwell's research showed the fifth wedding anniversary to be wood. Accordingly, he looked at a furniture store and found wooden beds, wooden chairs, wooden tables, but nothing that was perfect. He looked in a gift shop and found wooden bowls, wooden brushes, wooden bracelets. He looked in an import store and found wooden stools, wooden forks and spoons, wooden plates and stone figures. Hand-carved stone figures, almost half-sized.

Maxwell stared at one of the stone figures. Beth always gave gifts that were perfect without being correct. For a wedding present she gave him a radio-controlled airplane that he flew every day until it clipped some telephone wires and burned on the ground. For Christmas she had given him a Dallas Cowboys football helmet that he wore while watching television. On his birthday, she had given him a second-hand computer for his office at home to match the computer in his office at school. Perhaps the perfect fifth anniversary gift wasn't traditional wood but spontaneous stone.

There was no name on the bearded statue, but to Maxwell it looked like a young Socrates. Maxwell didn't know a lot about sculpture but young Socrates seemed well carved. His hands were outstretched, palms up in disputation, and if Beth didn't want him in the house she could put him in the garden with a large ashtray, a basket of dry flowers or a birdbath in his hands. She'd think of lots of ways to use him, he convinced himself. Socrates was attractive, utilitarian and inexpensive if he bought him without the sheep.

"That's Jesus," Beth exclaimed when he pulled the wrapping off the statue and wished her a happy anniversary.

Maxwell wasn't an agnostic, not exactly. Religion was one of those areas, like geology, that he considered decorative rather than fundamental. "It's Socrates," he apologized. "Or maybe Aristotle."

"It's Jesus. The beard. The outstretched hands. The robe."

If Beth said it was Jesus, it was Jesus. Beth knew Jesus. "Oh, yeah, now I see what you mean. It is Jesus." He shifted into the speech he had prepared. "You've made me happy for five years, happier than I have any right to be. I love you. And I wanted to give you something special."

"It's an idol."

"It's hand-carved. It came with some sheep." He should have known then; Socrates didn't hang out with sheep. "Maybe we can buy those later if you want. For your birthday."

"I can't have an idol in the house." She had the same disappointed, determined, loving look she was wearing when she said, "I can't marry you if you deny God."

The only time he had been in her church, their wedding, he hadn't looked around a lot but he had noticed that the stained glass windows had no figures at all, no people, no sheep, no nothing. Just fragments of stained glass. She agreed to go with him to his church if he would find one. They all seemed much the same to him, empiricist or existential, wood or stone with a cross on a spire or a cross without a spire. Finally, they agreed he would respect her religion and she would allow him time to think about religion and make up his mind. And he was still thinking about it. Well, he was still thinking about thinking about it.

"We'll say it's a young Socrates. Nobody knows what he looked like."

"Nobody knows what Jesus looked like either," Beth said. "But everyone agrees he looked like that."

"I'll take it back," he said, resigned to failure as a gift-giver.

"You can't take Jesus back. You don't even believe in Him."

Christianity was more complicated than he had thought. "Churches have statues."

"Not my church. If you want to join one of those churches, and really believe in it and support it, I'll . . . I'll go with you."

Marriage was more complicated than he thought. "I'll donate Jesus to one of those churches."

"You can't do that. It has to be consecrated or something."

Philanthropy was more — "What do you want me to do with it?"

She put her arms around him and buried her face in his shoulder. "I'm sorry, Max." The word "sorry" came slow and low and tugged at his heart. He wanted to please her so much. "I know you meant well, but I wouldn't feel right having an idol in the house."

"We could put it in the garden," he suggested.

"No exchanges, no returns," the manager of the store said. He looked even more determined than Beth. A thin lip curled with a hint of disapproval. A long hair hung from his nostril.

"Because you're a Christian?"

"Because I'm a businessman."

"Maybe I could exchange it for Socrates."

"We don't have Socrates."

"Who is that?" he asked, pointing at a statue.

"That's not anyone. That goes with the sheep."

"I thought Jesus went with the sheep."

"The sheep are separate items. You can buy them to go with that figure or with the figure you have. Or any figure in the store."

"Is this Jesus?" he asked, indicating the heavy stone in his arms.

"If you say so."

"Maybe I could exchange Jesus for some of the sheep."

"No exchanges, no returns."

"One sheep. Jesus, which cost a lot more, for one sheep."

It took a lot of deductive reasoning regarding natural law but he exchanged the figure for a recumbent sheep. The standing ones looked apt to fall and break something.

"That's Jesus," Beth exclaimed.

"It's a lamb."

"The lamb of God. Max, I'm sorry. I know you're trying to please me, and any other lamb would be okay. But not this one."

"A standing lam — sheep?" he asked.

⁓

"No exchanges, no returns," said the manager of the store.

"What am I supposed to do with this?"

"You might try Ty Streeter."

Ty Streeter, a local collector, would buy Jesus — "He'll buy anything," they laughed in the faculty club — but Max wasn't sure about the lamb. Besides, it was the principle of the thing. "I want the Jesus back. It cost more and I want it back."

Following philosophical discussion of social contracts and blind will, Maxwell carried Jesus to his car. Jesus was heavier than he had thought.

⁓

"The things I collect all shine; they glitter," Ty said, waving an arm encased in shiny material and a hand that glittered with gold. "They catch the eye. You hear what I'm saying?" One wall was covered by *The Last Supper,* the others by nude women with enormous breasts, children with enormous eyes and bullfighters sticking swords into enormous bulls, all painted on velvet. On the table and in the corners were gaunt Quixotes on even gaunter horses made from aluminum beer cans, suits of armor made of tin and wooden plaques bearing plastic bull's horns with what appeared to be real ears and tails.

"I wasn't asking you to buy it," Maxwell explained. "I don't have any need for it and I'd like you to have it."

"Jesus'd stick out here. Too rough hewn. There's no flash."

"Perhaps you know someone —"

"I'll level with you, okay? Most collectors are looking for something that fills the eye, you hear what I'm saying? There are a few looking for something that will tickle the belly, but most want something that when they look at it, they say, 'that's mine,' and that makes them feel good. This thing just . . . well, you own it. Does it make you feel proud? See what I'm saying?"

Selling the statue was out of the question. He had to find someone who would appreciate it as a gift, someone less particular. Margaret Cargile, who retired from the English Department last year. She lived alone and when she closed her office at the school, she took home not only her books and lectures but forty years of papers students had never bothered to pick up.

"Oh, I'd love to have it," Margaret exclaimed, patting Jesus on the head. "It would be perfect in my garden."

"That would be great," he said, looking around. Her house was almost on the street and a curved driveway used up her yard except for a tiny flowerbed along the front of the porch. Some garden. "It's pretty heavy, so tell me where you want it."

"In the garden," she said. "Behind the house."

He carried the statue through a hallway almost filled with stacks of books, magazines, newspapers, lecture notes. He glimpsed into one dark room and found it filled with furniture. Clothes were piled almost to the ceiling on the bed and chairs, spilled out of closets and hung from closet doors. She held a door open and he stepped into her backyard garden.

"Where?" he groaned, looking at a yard filled with bottles, dishes, horseshoes, Christmas wreaths, animal skulls, a bathtub, a kitchen sink, a toilet with flowers growing out of the tank and two tires. The only tree sported old license tags and more bottles.

"It's a bottle garden," she said. "And I see the perfect place for it in the flush toilet."

"This is Jesus," he said.

"Oh, I didn't realize it was Jesus. Maybe I could put it in the tree. Or was that Zacchaeus."

"If it fell, it could really hurt someone."

"Maybe I should put it in the house. Let me look for the perfect place."

Maxwell looked for a place to set the statue where he wouldn't have to bend over to pick it up again. The toilet seemed the only place. He struggled for a new grip on Jesus and leaned against the house, listening to Margaret making her way through the rooms.

"I'm sorry. I don't seem to have a place for it right now. Perhaps if you came back next week. I'll call."

"Sure-ah," he grunted, blundering his way down the hall leaving falling books and papers in his wake. He replaced the statue in the trunk of the car, straightened his cramped fingers and bent over to stretch his aching back. It'd be a miracle if Jesus didn't give him a hernia.

Now, what was he going to do with it? Where could he keep it for a week? Or, more likely, a month? Certainly not at home.

~

When he returned, Beth was cutting up vegetables. "We're having beef and stir-fry for lunch," she said. "Strawberries and ice cream for dessert." It was her way of apologizing for not being thrilled by his present.

"I'm sorry about the . . . the statue," he said, digging into the beef and stir-fry, his favorite.

"I know you were trying to please me. And you did. By taking it back," Beth said. "Would you let that be my present? Please?"

"Well, okay," he grumbled, secretly relieved. Maybe it was the thought that counted, like Christians said. He just wished that one time he could find something —

"Happy anniversary," she said, giving him a thin package when he had finished his dessert.

"What is it?" he asked, tearing off the wrapper and finding a computer game that allowed him to search for and destroy alien spacecraft. He had no computer games, considering them an extravagance for someone as serious-minded and with as little money and time as he had. He would never have bought one for himself, never admitted that he wanted one, but in his daydreams — "How did you know?" he asked.

"I just thought it was something you would like to have."

She had done it again. She had surprised and pleased him, fulfilling a dream. Why couldn't he ever do something like that for her? "I gave the statue to Margaret Cargile," he said, hoping to make her happy.

"I'm glad," Beth said. "But I wonder that she had room for it. Where did she put it?"

"She's looking for a place."

"Did you leave it with her? She can't move it by herself."

"I put it where, well, if someone takes it, what difference does it make? It'll be because they want it."

"Where did you put Him?"

All he wanted was to make his wife happy on their anniversary, to show how much she meant to him. Christians had invented gift-giving; he was certain of that. That's the way they punished their enemies. "I left it at the landfill."

"You took Jesus to the garbage dump?"

"It's not the garbage dump. It's outside the garbage dump. Anyone who goes by can see it and if they like it —"

"They'll think someone has discarded Jesus. They're not going to take it home. They're going to throw it in the garbage. I can't believe you did that. You promised to respect my religion."

"I'm trying. I didn't know how irrational it was."

"That doesn't sound like respect to me," she said.

"What do you want me to do with it? Just tell me and I'll do it."

"If you understood me, if you ever went to church with me, you wouldn't have bought it in the first place."

She was right of course. "I'm going to get the statue."

"Don't bring it home," she said.

He drove slowly to the landfill, allowing as much time as

possible for someone to find the statue and take it home. When he saw it was gone he whispered a prayer of thanksgiving. Someone, certainly some religious person, had taken it. He was sure of it. Perhaps a family. An honest, hard-working-but-not-neglectful man who always paid full price for groceries, his devoted-if-overweight-wife who knitted socks for children in Bangladesh, a precocious-but-not-sissy son who longed for Sunday School, a pretty-but-not-prissy daughter who read her Bible every night before going to bed. And that was what he was going to report to his wife.

As he started to drive away, he noticed a trash truck with two men in the back throwing things into the landfill. Before he could look away, he saw one of them throw out what might have been Jesus. He wasn't sure of it. He could drive away and tell his wife that some devout family had taken it and was, even now, admiring it in their —

If she ever discovered that he left Jesus in the garbage dump she would never forgive him. Well, she was a Christian, she would forgive, but she would never again see him as her "wise man bearing gifts," as she called him when he asked her to marry him. Just before she added, "But I can't marry you if you deny God."

Maxwell waited until the truck left, then got out and walked to the dump. It really was a dump. Clothes, broken furniture, old toys, even trash and garbage littered the ground and a fire burned at one edge. Beneath the garbage he could see one hand sticking up through tree branches.

Maxwell climbed down into the pit, picked his way through litter, dug Jesus out of the branches and took him to the car. Scarred but still intact. A few leaves and other debris. He carefully wiped off the statue and put it where he had left it before. This time he watched to be certain that some worthy-but-not-necessarily-wealthy family carried it away.

There seemed to be little traffic. He might have to wait for hours and there were papers to grade and next week's lectures to prepare. He would put the statue in his already cramped office; his wife couldn't complain about that. If one of his colleagues asked, he would explain that it was Socrates. Or Aristotle. Unless one of his colleagues from comparative religion recognized Jesus. Or someone from the art department.

Of course. The art department. Scott Bruner was a sculptor. He would appreciate the statue. Or he would know someone who would.

"You'll have to find someone who likes primitives," said Scott, who looked primitive himself in his sandals, frayed, beltless jeans and stained T-shirt.

"Primitives?"

"See the body symmetry," Scott said, digging into his crotch with a thumb. "Both hands extended exactly the same way. Sure sign of primitive art. But it's made of solid material, good stuff."

"Maybe you have some use for it," Maxwell suggested.

"I don't work much with stone," said Scott, hawking and spitting into a corner of the backyard shed that was filled with junk. "Too cold. I like found pieces, the detritus of contemporary life transformed into form and meaning." He turned the statue, studying the material. "I have students who would like to have this stone to work with."

"You mean, break it up?" He wasn't sure how Beth would feel about that. It was an idol, but it was still Jesus.

"They could practice on it."

"What would it look like?"

"I don't know. Whatever they saw in it."

"They'd cannibalize it, right? Turn it into dust?"

"Maybe. What were you going to do with it?"

He was going to leave it at the landfill. Still, he didn't like the idea of students chipping it into gravel. "I just thought something useful could be done with it."

"Well, leave it here and I'll see."

He did feel guilty about leaving it, but he got his wife a

hand-carved wooden bowl. He knew it wasn't perfect but Beth smiled and called him her wise man bearing gifts, after he reported that Scott wanted the statue. At least he didn't let that shyster salesman get away with palming off a cheap sheep on him.

⁓

Maxwell had forgotten about Jesus when the doorbell rang one day. Scott was at the door. Apparently wearing the same clothes. "Here's your stone," he said, handing Maxwell a large box. "I worked on it some but it's yours and I wanted you to have it back."

"Is it a lamb?" Max asked without opening the box.

Scott looked doubtful. "Okay, it's a lamb."

"Maybe a lion?"

"If you want it to be a lion, it's a lion."

"What do you think it is?" Max asked.

"I don't have any need to reduce experience to words."

"This is not an experience. This is a thing," Max insisted, hefting the box containing the lighter but still solid stone. "What is it?"

"If you put it behind your door, it's a doorstop. If you put it in your garden, it's a statue. If you put it in a museum, it's art."

"Okay," Max resigned. "What did it mean when you were doing it?"

"Art doesn't mean, art is. It's what I do. You gave me stone and this is what I did. If you don't like it, give it away."

Maxwell watched Scott's stained T-shirt disappear down the sidewalk.

"Who was that?" Beth asked behind him.

"That was Scott. From the art department." Mistaking illogical for inscrutable, he added under his breath.

"Why didn't you ask him in?"

"He was. . . . He gave me this."

She opened the box and took out the carved stone. "It's beautiful," she said. "He just gave it to you?"

"I gave him the statue, remember? And he . . . he gave me this."

"I hope you thanked him."

"I didn't know exactly what to say."

"I love it," she said.

"You do?"

"The contrast between the rugged and the smooth. The way it defines everything around it, both space and matter." Maybe he should have taken an art history class in addition to aesthetics. "I know exactly where to put it. In the living room where everyone can see it."

"You'll have to tell them what it is," Maxwell pointed out.

"It's love, silly. Don't you see?"

"It looks more like a bowl or a cup. Except that it's got a hole in the bottom." Representing insatiability. Endless appetite.

"Because it never stops giving." She placed the stone on the table in the middle of the living room and stepped back to admire it. Then she put her arms around his neck and hugged him. "You had it made for me, didn't you?"

"Well, not exactly."

"I can tell by the way you're acting. You know me so well," she said, kissing him. "And it's the nicest present anyone ever gave me."

"Better than the punch bowl Shirley gave you?"

"I've always preferred your gifts."

"The vacuum cleaner? The trip to Las Vegas?"

"Because you gave them to me."

Maxwell accepted her hugs and kisses while he pondered the stone that wasn't at all the gift he had given her. Well, maybe it wasn't what he intended but it was what he meant.

X-Mas

I knowed something was wrong. I could feel it in the air. I could tell by the way the cattle was acting. The sheep was acting funny too, but you can't tell nothing by sheep. Sheep are always seeing something that no one else sees. Show me a man who listens to sheep and I'll show you a man who spends all his time building fences.

Now, a horse is sensible, except when it comes to another horse, and Bob had his neck out and his ears up like the sheep did. I looked over where Cletis was riding Sweetpea, and him and Sweetpea looked like Bob. I always thought Cletis and Sweetpea looked a lot alike anyhow; both of them got that close-eyed, long-faced look like they was better than what they was doing. Cletis must be fifty, near as old as me, and he ain't never been nothing but a pick-up hand, working at four or five different ranches. He's a good one, the only one I ever use, and he could be foreman if he wasn't always right.

Me and Cletis had been out since daylight checking the stock. Folks think it don't get cold in South Texas and it don't until everybody thinks it can't and then it does. A norther blows in and freezes everything. Sometimes it freezes into ice; when it don't the wind is so cold you can't tell the difference. Why, I've seen snow. It's usually gone by midday, but folks and animals suffer if they're not prepared for it. That's why me and Cletis was out. We was moving the stock out of the wind and feeding them so they didn't suffer none.

When we was done I was ready to load up the horses, get in the truck and head for the house. The heater in the truck hadn't worked in four years but it was out of the wind. But Cletis stood around like he was sniffing the air. "I got me a funny feeling," he said.

"What kind a funny feeling," I asked him.

"If I knowed that it wouldn't be funny, would it? It'd just be a feeling. Like frozen ears is a feeling." Cletis wasn't born more than fifteen miles from where I was, but he was in the army once and he thought that made him smarter than anybody. Shoot, all he learned in the army was how to march. He told me so himself. "Cletis," I sometimes say to him, "since you was in the army, march down to the corral and close the gate."

"Let's run by the hunters' trailer," I said, but there wasn't nothing at the hunters' trailer, not even a hunter, 'cause it was Christmas Day and they was all home sitting by the fire watching football.

"You think we ought to check the first house?" Cletis asked. Cletis was in the army and he thinks he knows more about duty than anybody. "Cletis," I sometimes say to him, "there's more to duty than killing rattlesnakes."

"I reckon we have to," I said. I don't know why he asked about the old house. It was way back in Whiskey Rock Canyon and in the opposite direction where I wanted to be. It was the old first house of the ranch, a two-room bare-wall cabin with whatever shingles and floor the wind and rats hadn't gotten. It never had running water or electricity and the only heat was from the old fireplace, but sometimes during deer season on a rainy day hunters would duck into it for a couple of hours, which was about all a body could stand. And sometimes wets drifting through the country looking for a job used it to get out of the wind. They never bothered nothing, but Mr. Hasslocker didn't like them staying there. He was afraid they'd steal something or eat one of his cows. Shoot, I ain't never seen a wet that wouldn't put a banker to shame when it come to honest. But we was supposed to run them off. Them was our orders.

I pulled up in front of the cabin. We couldn't see no smoke from the chimbley or nothing, but we both knowed somebody was in there; a house with somebody in it just don't feel like a house that's empty. Even a horse knows that. And, whoever it was, we was going to have to turn them out into the cold. And on Christmas Day. I turned and looked at Cletis. "Your Spanish is better than mine," I said. Cletis grew up talking Tex-Mex like me but he pretends he forgot how in the army. "Tell them to vamoose."

"Tell them yourself. You're the foreman."

The only time Cletis remembers I'm boss is when there's something he don't want to do. So I got out of the truck and walked over to the door and shoved it open. There ain't never been no doorknob but the doorjamb is warped and friction keeps it closed. I stepped in and it took a minute for my eyes to adjust to the dimness, but all I could see was a pile of rags in a corner. Them hunters is all coat-and-tie folks in the city, but when they come out here they wear the raggediest things they got and when they get tired of carrying them, they just drop them wherever they are. Then I made out a girl, and a boy was standing in front of her kind of protecting her, and he was saying something to me that I didn't understand. "Cletis, get in here," I yelled.

"What's going on?" Cletis asked when he got inside. He

palavered with the boy for a while and then he turned to me and said that the boy was apologizing for being in the cabin but they couldn't find no other place and the girl was having a baby.

"Baby?" Sure enough, there was a little old baby wrapped up in what was either a flannel shirt or the stuffing out of a sleeping bag.

"What is it?"

"Boy."

"Don't that beat all that they'd walk out of Mexico with a baby on the way."

"They ain't from Mexico," Cletis said. "They're them kind of people that nobody wants and everybody keeps running off. Salvadories or something like that."

"Well, they come to the right place to get run off," I said. "There ain't no place for them here." Cletis acts tough because he was in the army, but I knew he wasn't going to throw no woman and baby out in the cold, and he wasn't going to say much if I didn't. He turned and walked out the door. "Where you going?" I asked him.

"I'm going to chop some wood, you dumb horse jockey. The baby's blue from the cold, and the mama's teeth are chattering."

I followed him out and picked up the chips and got a fire going and helped him carry in wood, and then we kneeled on the floor because it was too cold to sit, and tried to thaw out. "Look at them shoes," Cletis said. They weren't really shoes; they were them kind of sandals them folks wear.

"How far you reckon they come?" I said.

"A far piece," Cletis says. "But not as far as they got to go. There ain't no home for folks like them."

"What about the baby? Ain't there no place for him?"

Cletis gave me one of them army looks that's supposed to mean he has seen something I ain't. I threw some more wood on the fire and got it to going where we could stand back a ways and let it warm up the room. I watched the mama and daddy in the firelight. They was scared, you could see that, but kind of brave too. I guess you'd have to be to come as far as they had.

It got warm enough that the mama unwrapped the baby a little and I could see him. Leastways, I could see his head. He wasn't much to look at. His eyes was squinched closed and his mouth was puckered like life needed a bit more seasoning to suit his taste. And his hands was knotted up with a fist full of nothing. I didn't look at him long. When it comes to babies, give me a pig ever time. Some folks like lambs, but a newborn lamb looks spindly and all legs. A pig is handsome from the time it's born until it's near a year old. With humans it's the other way around. They're borned ugly and some of them never get pretty. "Hey, Clete, ain't much to look at, is he?"

"He looks like a baby," Clete said, but he hadn't never seen a real baby before neither. Like me, all he'd seen was foals and calves and lambs and things that already got hair on them.

Then the baby began sticking his tongue out and his face shriveled up and his fists started to shake and he kind a bleated. His mama shook him around and held him close, and I got scared. "You think he's gonna die, Clete?" I hadn't never doctored nothing but animals except for that time a bull near stepped Cletis' ear off and I sewed it back on for him. And he held a mirror and complained the whole time that the seam wasn't straight. His ear does pucker a little but he always wears a hat anyhow and the only time you can tell it is when he gets a haircut.

"He made it this far, didn't he?" Clete said, and I knowed he was thinking about all the miles them folks had brought that baby to be borned in this place. That kid shore had him some tough parents. You have to wonder if they didn't think there was something wrong, them coming this far and still not finding no good place for a baby to be born.

"What do you reckon will happen to him? He ain't one of

us, and folks are always gonna be wishing he had stayed where he belonged and not come trying to take away what's rightfully ours."

"You can't never tell," Clete said. "When you're little like that, you can be anything."

"Here we are looking at this little baby that don't look like nothing appetizing; wouldn't it be something if he growed up to be somebody? Why, he might go back wherever he come from and be a leader of his country. And you wanted to run him off like he wasn't nothing better than a wet."

"I didn't want to run him off."

"You shore would have if Mr. Hasslocker told you to, you would. Why, you could a gone down in history books as a bad man."

"What about you?" Cletis said.

I got a good eye for horses and cows and I ain't often wrong about people, but it does seem hard to expect a man to cull kids. I bet there ain't one in ten could look at that kid and tell whether he was worth keeping or not. I reckon we was all thinking the same, 'cause the mama and daddy was looking at each other like they wondered what they had got themselves into. Cletis was staring at the fire and snorting like a bull that's done sulled. I got up.

"Where you going?" Cletis asked.

"I'm going to take the horses back to the house and turn them loose. Then I'm going to see if I can rustle up some grub. I ain't et, and I bet these folks ain't neither."

"Bring some water," he said. "And something to heat it in, and some rags. And don't tell nobody." I didn't even answer him. I ain't stupid.

Well, dang if Mr. Hasslocker didn't call when I was back at the house trying to get things together. Leave it to a man who lives in the city to worry himself on a cold night. Sometimes I think he worries more about the stock than I do. I told him we'd moved them and fed them. He asked if everything else was okay. I ain't no hand at lying, so I tried to haw around it and he kept on until I had to tell him there was a woman and a baby in the first house and they couldn't leave. I didn't say much about the daddy. I figured the less said about him, the better.

"They got no business with my property," he said. "Soon as they're able I want them out of that house." He don't take care of the house or nothing, and I bet he ain't seen it in ten years. Shoot, he ain't been on the ranch since spring shearing, but it's his cabin and he can do what he wants to with it. And if he don't want nobody in it, then there ain't going to be nobody in it. That's the law, I reckon.

I got together some pans that I didn't mind putting in the fire and a whole bunch of can goods. And I took my blanket and the only clean sheet, and the bottle of wine me and Cletis was going to have with Christmas dinner.

When I got back to the cabin, Cletis and the daddy had chopped some more wood and moved it into the house, enough to last all night. Cletis had been talking to the daddy some more and he said they hadn't had no fire because they didn't have no matches, and that the baby's name was Manuel, and that they had been walking for more than a year.

I put some water in a pan and warmed it and the mama washed the baby and wrapped him up in my good blanket. She didn't want to rip up the sheet so I done it for her, and showed her she was supposed to use it for diapers. She thought I wanted the baby, and she handed him to me, but I ain't never changed no baby so I gave him back.

After the mama and baby settled down for the night, I divided the wine into three pans because I forgot to bring cups. Me and Cletis and the daddy drank our wine, and ever once in a while one of us would throw a log in the fire. We sat up all night. We didn't talk much because we was men and there wasn't a whole lot to say. This wasn't their place, never was and never would be. They might just as well turn around and go back where they come from for all the good they done.

I thought a lot that night about things I never had no cause to think of before. I thought about when I was a baby and my mama and daddy wondered what they had. I bet they never thought their son might grow up and be foreman of a big ranch like this. Why, for all they knowed they could a been holding a criminal or a president, although I don't think I'd ever made a president. My daddy told me, "You can show or you can shovel," and he never had a lot of respect for folks that made a spectacle of themselves.

The next day three hunters showed up. Mr. Hasslocker had told them about the baby in the first house and they had to see for themselves. They all three had flat, white, washed faces and smelled like toilet water. One was a banker, and one was a lawyer, and the other one got rich buying and selling companies he didn't own. They warmed themselves by the fire and said what a fine looking baby it was, which was a lie, and how glad they was to see him, which was another.

They clowned around with the baby and made remarks about the mama and daddy and got to joking among themselves about how they ought to give the baby a present seeing as how he was borned on Christmas Day. They was just showing off, amusing themselves. The banker give him a dollar. "So he'll never be broke," he said. The lawyer give him a pocket can-opener, "so he'll never go hungry," and the other one give him one of them little radios you put in your ear, "so he'll always know what's going on."

They looked at me and Cletis like we was too dumb to think of something funny to give him. We didn't say nothing and they got to looking at each other like it was time to do something manful, and they went off to shoot them a trophy they could hang on the wall back in San Antonio.

Me and Cletis went back to work. That was the last I seen of them Salvadories. I don't know what happened to them. All I know is, something was wrong. From the beginning, I knowed something was wrong. Even the horses knew that.

Peace

Games Children Play

Her children were at the window again, peeking in, trying to gain a glimpse of her, tapping on the glass to get her attention. "Come out," they called. "We have a surprise for you." Rose pretended not to hear them. She wasn't going to turn and look at them and she wasn't going out. She knew their games. She wasn't going to let them in the house either. When she let them in they took things. The last time they took her.

"It's me, Mother. Your daughter, Sissie. And this is my husband, Arnold, the one who took over Dad's car dealership. And there is your son, Bucky. Don't you remember Bucky? And his wife, Helen, the one who boils everything? And look what I've got."

Rose peeked while pretending not to know they were

there. Sissie had a birthday cake. "Don't you want to see what else I've got?"

"Look," Arnold said. He pointed at a card table covered with orange paper. The table was circled by five chairs. Each chair was topped with a little white and orange sun umbrella. Helen and Bucky were sitting at the table waving. Across the street Mr. Binkley was looking out his window, wondering what was going on.

"It's your birthday," Arnold said.

Rose knew it was her birthday. Did they think she was so old she couldn't remember her own birthday?

"We have a present for you." Arnold held a brightly wrapped package beside his head and shook it. His face was as close to having an expression as she had ever seen it.

At the table Helen held up a package and opened her eyes wide and made an "O" with her mouth. "Don't you want to see what we got you?" Helen called.

She didn't. Her horoscope said, "Your duty may require travel; powerful acquaintances are nearby."

She remembered the time they brought her a cake and then ate it all themselves. They gave her an electric barbecue grill and a travel coffeepot, then a year later said, "You don't need these," and took them back. Who reared such children?

"Please come out," Sissie said. "Please, Mother."

They knew how it affected her when they called her "Mother," but she wasn't their mother anymore. They never listened to her advice. They wouldn't let her cook for them, not after she burned the timer, and when they came in the house they rearranged her dishes and furniture and threw away things she wanted to keep. "What do you want with this old magazine? If you haven't read it by now you never will." They threw away her sourdough starter because it smelled sour. "I'm going to throw away this medicine. All it does is make you drowsy."

She had become their child. That's how they treated her,

like a child. Telling her that Shady Oaks cafeteria had the best hamburgers in town. And she wasn't going to go outside and play their game.

Behind her she could hear Sissie and Arnold discussing how to deal with her. "Do you think she's pouting?" Sissie asked.

"I don't know," Arnold said, "she's your mother. Maybe your brother should talk to her. Bucky's fifty years old; it's time he faced up to his mother. If you can get him away from the food long enough."

"If you had to eat Helen's cooking you'd be at the table too," Sissie said. "I wonder how many times she boiled the asparagus."

"I thought it was her spinach dip."

"She said it was 'asparagus crunch.' "

"It's time you stopped being big sister and made Bucky carry some of the responsibility," Arnold said.

"Mother, Bucky's eating the chicken and you know how much you like my baked chicken. I made it especially for you, and if you don't come out he's going to eat it all. Bucky, you better save some of that chicken for your mother," Sissie yelled, shaking a finger at him.

Bucky hunched over his plate and pretended to be stuffing his mouth with baked chicken. Rose's children were embarrassing her in front of her neighbors. Down the street Mrs. Labatt was sweeping her sidewalk, and Mrs. Labatt never swept her sidewalk.

"Don't you worry, Mother Rose," Helen yelled, waving hands that were as big and dry as her biscuits. Rose had never been able to understand why Bucky would marry a woman with dry hands. Not that she didn't like her daughter-in-law, but it was just like Bucky to marry the tallest girl in the class and then not grow up.

"There's plenty here for everyone," Helen yelled, holding Rose's picnic hamper, the one her husband had given her when the children were babies. "We're going to do things with our children when they are young so they will do things with us when they are old," he had said. What they did was take things. "What are you going to do with a picnic hamper?" Bucky said. And Helen took it. "Mother, I don't want you taking these vitamins anymore. Arnold can use them." Arnold had given up food and cigarettes in favor of vitamins and jogging. He was thin, healthy and tiresome. He had always been tiresome but now he was tiresome on a different subject.

"Help yourself to the asparagus but save a drumstick for me," Arnold yelled, pushing against the side of the house to stretch his calves.

If John were still alive the children wouldn't be out there on the lawn putting on a show for the whole neighborhood to see; she was sure of that. He would tell them, "Get the hell away from my house." That's what he had told Arnold when Arnold tried to take over the dealership so John could have more time. "I don't want more time," John had told him. "And if you think you can take over the dealership while I'm alive you can just get the hell away from my house." But John had listened to Sissie. John listened to everyone; that's what Rose had loved about him. He always listened when she read her horoscope aloud and he made suggestions about how to improve her probabilities.

Arnold turned toward the table, pulled his ears and yelled, "Stone deaf."

They thought she was deaf because sometimes she pretended not to hear. "Don't you think you should let Bucky sell the house for you? It's just too much for you to keep up." "Wouldn't you be happier in a nice nursing home with people your age?"

At first Rose had argued with them and they left angry and talked before her grandchildren about how cranky she had gotten. So she started pretending she didn't hear them and they decided she was deaf and took her stereo and telephone. “She can’t hear on the telephone,” Helen said. “She thinks everything is an obscene call.”

It did seem like an obscene telephone call. Why did her children give her a pink sewing machine anyway? And if he was a sewing machine repairman why didn’t he identify himself instead of, when she answered the telephone, saying, “Your old pinkie’s ready.” She had been so startled she dropped the telephone. Afraid to pick it up again she ran next door and called Sissie to come right away. Because she was breathless from running and being startled, Sissie thought she was having a heart attack and called Bucky, who was a high school principal and highly excitable. Bucky called an ambulance.

Bucky and Sissie arrived before the ambulance and found her clutching her breast and staring at the telephone that was emitting her name. Bucky picked up the receiver, said, “Okay,” and hung up. “Your sewing machine is ready,” he said. “I’ll pick it up for you.”

“Are you okay?” Sissie had asked her.

“Of course I’m okay. I . . . I thought it was an obscene telephone call.”

“Mr. Sorenson?” Bucky asked.

“What did he say?” Sissie wanted to know.

“He said my old pinkie was ready.”

Sissie hid her face behind one hand and she and Bucky smirked at each other like naughty schoolchildren.

Believing she couldn’t hear, her children walked into her house without ringing the doorbell. She expected Bucky; he came almost every day for lunch. But Rose had been so startled to find Sissie behind her, she gasped. “It’s me, Mother,” Sissie had screamed. “Don’t you recognize your own daughter?”

When Rose asked Sissie what she was doing, Sissie said she had come to clean her mother’s house — Sissie, who had never cleaned her own room and had once lost her telephone in her bed. It had taken forever to teach her to blow her nose and when she learned, Sissie blew her nose on the curtains, the minister's robe and her father's suit. But Sissie didn't remember that; she could only remember when she was president of the Junior League.

"Do you think she is just going to sit there all day and not even know we're out here celebrating her birthday?" Arnold asked.

"I don't know where her mind is anymore," Sissie said. "I knew something was wrong when she started singing along with the choir."

How did Sissie think she could sing along with the choir if she was deaf? Of course Sissie had always believed whatever she wanted to. When she was in high school she thought everybody hated her because she was runner-up for Homecoming Queen. She had believed Arnold was smart although she had to help him with his school work. She thought he was exciting because he had grease under his nails, drove an old car he had put together himself and smoked cigarettes. Now Sissie believed Arnold was a success because he gave her a new car every year, although she knew that if her father hadn't been a car dealer, Arnold would be working in a garage.

It made Rose feel closer to John to hum along with the choir. John was singing in the choir when he fell over dead between "Hallelujah" and "Amen." John was a lusty singer. She would be eternally grateful she had married a religious man. It had given him something to be mad at besides his wife.

"You'd think she would want to be with people her age," Sissie said. "When she was at Shady Oaks, she won the bridge tournament and was in the final round of checkers."

"She probably cheated the way she cheated the children," Arnold said.

She only cheated when playing with the children. In the beginning she had cheated so they would win. They were always so surprised and happy. "I beat Grandma, I beat Grandma," they shouted. She didn't care who won; she just wanted them to be happy. Then a few years later she overheard Arnold, Jr., telling his mother, "I landed on Boardwalk and I didn't have to pay anything."

"Now, dear," Sissie had said, "Your grandmother is forgetful. You should let her win sometimes."

Rose never let him win again. When he wanted to bet his money against John's collection of miniature cars, she beat him. She had told him he could have the cars when she died, but like his father he didn't want to wait for what he was going to get. She cleaned him out, although she had to cheat a little. It wasn't the money; she wanted to teach Arnold, Jr., a lesson — the same lesson John should have taught Arnold, Sr., no matter what Sissie said. Wait until it was given to him.

"I've been worried to death about her since she burned the timer," Sissie said.

Bucky preferred his mother's cooking to the school cafeteria and came to her house for lunch almost every day. She didn't mind; it gave her something to do. One day she put a roast in the oven, intending to clean her closets until Bucky came. She found things she had forgotten she had, Bucky didn't come and when Sissie came looking for him the roast was burned and the kitchen full of smoke. Rose tried to explain that she had lost track of time expecting Bucky to interrupt her, but Sissie and Bucky gave each other that knowing look that she and John used to exchange over the children, and Helen gave her a timer.

Which was nice of her; Rose admitted that and always had. And no one tried to take it back. Somehow, when she put the meat loaf in the oven, she must have picked up the timer too. It was not in the meat loaf, no matter what Helen said. When Bucky came for lunch, the house was filled with smoke and Rose was sitting in the kitchen holding the timer, which had melted out of shape. "If I had a hammer and screwdriver I believe I could fix this thing," she said. She meant it as a joke. She meant she would like to hammer the thing to pieces.

Bucky didn't laugh. He talked to Sissie and Sissie had taken Rose to a restaurant. At the restaurant Sissie explained that she and Bucky were concerned for her safety and wanted Rose to choose a retirement home. Sissie spoke slowly and much too loudly for Rose's comfort.

Rose was not upset; they brought it up frequently and she had been considering it. However, Sissie made it clear that she wanted a decision right then. Rose wanted to think it over and excused herself to go to the ladies' room. She was unfamiliar with the restaurant and walked into the kitchen instead. George Cortez, who used to mow her lawn, was chef and was preparing Roast Duckling Montmorency, her specialty. They talked about the time George repaired the lawn mower and John had promised him a job when he finished high school. George said he didn't want to be a mechanic; he wanted to be a cook and own his own restaurant.

"Next year I'm opening my own restaurant and I want you to be my first customer," George told Rose.

Sissie found Rose in the kitchen, sampling the duckling, instructing George on adding cherries and butter to the claret and ordering his assistant to add more cornstarch. Sissie had been embarrassed that Rose had taken over the kitchen and rushed her from the restaurant without giving her time to explain.

The next time Sissie came, Arnold, Helen and Bucky were with her. They wanted to take her to get a hamburger and agreed that the best hamburgers in town were in the Shady Oaks cafeteria. At Shady Oaks Retirement Home, she was not surprised when Sissie said they had agreed it was time for her to move to a safer place and assured her this was it. Her horoscope had read, "Your family is about to make a big announcement. Have lunch at a new place or try a new product."

"But I don't have any clothes," Rose said. "I didn't bring my things."

"They're in the car," Arnold said.

"Please try it, Mother," Sissie said.

Rose looked at Bucky but Bucky looked away. Bucky was a high school principal and spent his life trying not to make people mad.

Rose didn't want to embarrass her children before strangers so she had agreed to stay for a while to see if she liked it. She liked it fine. She found a group of ladies who studied their horoscopes over breakfast, not that they believed in such things, but it was fun to talk about. She played bridge, learned macrame and origami and exercised every day.

She enjoyed not having to worry about cooking and dusting, but she wanted her things about her. Her favorite chair, the letters John sent when he was in the war, the children's and grandchildren's drawings, colorings and scribbling, her favorite books that she wouldn't reread but wanted to keep by her side, her cup and saucer — the only ones left of her wedding set, the bed she had slept in since she was a bride.

She missed her things the way she missed her wedding dress which she had let Sissie borrow. She didn't know what Sissie did on her wedding night and she didn't want to know, but when she got her wedding dress back the hem was ripped out and there was a stain and she just threw it away and never said another word about it. Not to this day had she said one word about Sissie ruining it or asked her why she helped Arnold fix his car in a wedding dress. Although it did look like Arnold could have rented a car for the occasion.

And she wanted to see the house again, before it was sold. Just to see it. She told the children what she wanted but they said there wasn't time, wasn't room, couldn't find what she wanted or didn't know. One day her horoscope said, "Don't expect unimaginative types to understand your daring plan. You end a productive day in confusion about money and family matters but you can finish your assignments if you take care of nutrition and get some rest."

That seemed auspicious and during visiting hours after

lunch she walked out the front door and started down the road to find a telephone to call a cab. The telephone was in a bar.

It was hot, she was thirsty and asked for a drink. The bartender gave her a beer. It wasn't what she intended but it tasted good. She asked the bartender what kind it was and found that he was from Quanah and he knew John's nephew and was in high school with the son of John's best friend, who would have been best man at her wedding if he could have gotten a leave from the army.

She forgot all about calling a cab until Sissie came in the bar. Bucky and Helen had gone to Shady Oaks to visit Rose and, finding her missing, had called the police, the sheriff's department and Sissie. Sissie found her; Sissie, who once lost her children in the bamboo and her geranium in the den.

Sissie took her back to Shady Oaks and told Bucky and Helen that Rose had spent the afternoon in a bar. Bucky had threatened to sue Shady Oaks for lacking proper supervision, the manager of the nursing home refused to take Rose back because she was an alcoholic who slipped off to a bar whenever they left her alone, and Helen said they would take her to Twilight Village, which was cheaper and better supervised. Sissie said her mother was not going to Twilight Village. Arnold said it wasn't Twilight Village, it was Twixt-Two Homes.

Rose was embarrassed by her children and tried to explain but no one would listen to her horoscope. Bucky agreed to pay for closer supervision and Shady Oaks agreed to take Rose back if she went to their AA meetings instead of origami.

Rose learned her lesson and when her horoscope read, "Underlying problem with property comes to light. Exciting events are becoming the norm but care in traveling will get you there. Little trips can turn into lengthy journeys," she pretended she was visiting a friend at the nursing home and a nice minister had volunteered to take her home. Sure enough, everything was just as she left it. Maybe Arnold, Jr., had learned his lesson. And the others as well.

It felt so good being home among her things that she decided to stay a while, just a little while, and enjoy them. She had scarcely been through the house when the children arrived, knocking, ringing her doorbell, begging her to let them in. She had refused but here they were again today. She should not have left so near her birthday.

"Mama Rose, yoo hoo. Happy birthday," Helen yelled, waving her big, dry hands. "Bucky, I don't believe she recognizes me. Mama Rose, it's me, Helen. I'm your daughter-in-law. And this is your son, Bucky. Don't you remember Bucky? Don't you want to come out and see your birthday cake? And blow out the candles? And see what else we brought you? You talk to her, Bucky, she doesn't know who I am."

"Mama, it's Bucky, your little boy. Mama, come and see your cake."

He was yelling for the whole neighborhood to hear. How was she ever going to explain her children's behavior? "I know who you are," she yelled at the window. "But I am not coming outside. And get those awful chairs off my lawn."

"She doesn't like the chairs," Helen said.

"She heard me," Bucky said.

"Of course I heard you. Everyone in the neighborhood heard you."

"Mama, let us in the house."

"No. When I let you in the house you take things."

"When did we ever take anything?" Helen asked.

"That's my picnic basket."

"What do you want with a picnic basket?"

It was hopeless. "And my telephone."

"I took your telephone because you can't hear," Helen said.

"I can't hear when you talk to me like a child, but I hear you just fine when you talk to me like your mother."

"Mother, will you come out?" Bucky asked.

"I'm not going to sit under that silly umbrella for all the neighbors to see."

"May we come in? We need to talk. To be sure everything is okay."

"Are we going to talk or are you going to talk to me?"

"We'll talk. And we'll listen. We are not going to take you to Shady Oaks without your consent."

Too bad it was Bucky who promised, the weakest of the lot. "Then you can come in. But we'll not talk in front of the neighbors, and if you start talking to me like a child, I'm going to stop listening."

She unlocked the door and they came in, carrying the cake and presents and sat down looking like bad children who expected a scolding. "Aren't you going to sing 'Happy Birthday'?" she asked.

"Mother, we want you to be safe," Sissie said.

Safe? When had she ever been safe? Or John either. They had always been afraid of losing the dealership, the house. The children. "I've never been safe. I've always been afraid, afraid that something would happen to you, that you wouldn't turn out the way I wanted. I've been afraid of growing old because I was afraid you couldn't manage without me."

Sissie was crying. Sissie, the strong one. And Helen, the big one. The children were afraid of her growing old, more afraid than she was. Life was scary but every day for all those years she had faced down her fears. And she had to keep on the way she had always done, the way she and John had done.

The children looked at each other, but this time she didn't mind the look. "We love you, Mother," Sissie said. "That hasn't changed, but what we need from you has changed."

She knew. They no longer needed her okay, her advice, her cooking. They could select their own clothes. They didn't need her to baby-sit anymore. They needed her to play her best against the children and win when she could do so without cheating. "What I need from you has also changed," she said. "I need you to listen when I talk," she said, promising herself that she wouldn't lecture them or read her horoscope aloud. "I would like you to recognize that my things belong to me." They ducked their heads and looked at each other. "I need you to respect my right to be foolish sometimes and wrong-headed and forgetful."

"I'll return the telephone," Helen said.

"I have your food processor," Sissie said.

"I don't want them," she said. Why didn't they listen? "I want the right to have them. I want the right to give them away to whomever I wish. Helen, I want to give you the telephone. And Sissie, I want to give you the food processor."

"Thank you, Mother," they said, like polite children, the kind of children a parent could be proud of. And they left like children who honored their parents. She just wished that Mr. Binkley and Mrs. Labatt had seen the way they acted in the house instead of the way they argued over how to remove the table and chairs from her yard.

When the house was quiet again, she went through it, deciding what she wanted to keep. If there wasn't room for her things at Shady Oaks, Sissie would have to keep some of them and exchange them when she visited.

She wanted Arnold, Jr., to have John's miniature car set. Helen and Sissie could go through the jewelry and take what they wanted and divide the rest between their daughters. She wanted her bed in her room at Shady Oaks. The rest of the furniture they could divide.

Before she called Bucky to take her back to Shady Oaks, she went through her things, one by one, enjoying them for a moment, then giving them away. It was one of the happiest days of her life.

A Second Chance

Ernest Evans awakened to bright lights, a white tunnel, his parents waiting for him. His mother seemed no longer angry at him for putting her in a nursing home, but his father looked as unforgiving as ever about the loan.

Ernest turned his back on his parents. They were dead, and he didn't want to be with them. He was only fifty; there were too many things he hadn't done, like taking the kids to Disneyland or his wife to San Francisco. He had promises to keep. He clutched at the white walls but there was no wall. He dug his feet into the floor but there was no floor. He looked over his shoulder. His parents were closer than before and Benny was standing with them. His old pal Benny seemed happy to see him.

Aware of his abnormal situation, Ernest recognized his

need for irregular remedy. Ernest was not unacquainted with religion. As a boy he had gone to Sunday School, sent by his parents. He had gotten married in the church at the insistence of his mother-in-law. He had sent his children to church until they were big enough to refuse. Church was a cultural exercise like softball. Everyone should be introduced to it but only children continued beyond a few symbolic pitches at Fourth of July picnics and other celebrations. Now it was bottom of the fifth in the Blue Ribbon Company City Championship and he had to hit a grand slam or the game would be called on the ten-run rule.

Ernest had lost faith in God's control of men and events when God's team, the Dallas Cowboys, lost the Super Bowl to the morally inferior and spiritually repugnant Pittsburgh Steelers. If God couldn't win the Super Bowl, how did He expect to win World War III against the Communists, who were little better than the Steelers? Nevertheless, Ernest still believed in God's control over life and death and put his faith to the test.

"Dear God," Ernest prayed. He had never addressed God before except in reciting church- or parent-prescribed pleas and in latter-day curses directed at labor officials, government regulations and Benny, and he assumed a businesslike approach was best. "It has come to my attention that Your future plans for me require not only a change in position but a change in residence. Such changes would put an undue burden on my family and, also, myself." Ernest thought it expeditious to put his family first; God rewarded unselfishness.

"Therefore, I wish to amend the terms and conditions of Your standard policy due to the unexpectedness of Your proposal. The transaction of this improvement in the terms of the contract would provide me with an opportunity to withdraw from business activities, put in order my financial affairs and make arrangements for the comfort and security of my family." That seemed conscientious enough to please God, who expected a man to take care of his wife and other unfortunates.

Next he needed a forceful claim. "I have always been a good man." Strong enough and not too bold for a man in his situation if he could support it with solid references. He had bought his son a car when he graduated from high school and made him a vice-president of the company when he finished college. He would put Terry at the top of his list of references. Terry wouldn't still be angry about Disneyland, not after all these years.

He had bribed safety inspectors for less than he paid for Jenny's church wedding. He made Bill, her husband, a vice-president and gave her a station wagon. Bill would be high on his list of references. Jenny didn't hold grudges; she had forgiven him for forbidding her to date that Japanese exchange student, not permitting her to study business and not giving her a job. She was smarter than Bill or Terry, but he knew Jenny. She would stop at nothing to be president and he had promised that job to Terry the day he was born.

Maybe Margie should be his third reference, ahead of Jenny. He and Margie had been married for almost thirty years; she had never been without a house and car and he had never been unfaithful. Margie appreciated that and so did God who wanted man to reproduce himself but didn't intend him to let it interfere with work, which is what he had told Terry. He wished Terry would marry, have kids and forget about sex, as he and Bill had done.

Unlike his father, Margie didn't carry a grudge. She knew that if he hadn't postponed their wedding and canceled their honeymoon to San Francisco Benny would have been president of the company. If Ernest hadn't looked after her interests and her children's, Benny's sons would be vice-presidents instead of Terry and Bill. Margie knew that and she had accepted his promise to take her to San Francisco when the business stabilized. And with Terry and Bill as vice-presidents and his withdrawing from business activities, that would be very soon. Assuming his proposal met with God's approval.

Four references — five if he decided to trust his mother, who said she would never forgive him for putting her in a nursing home and for tying her cat to the bumper — and all family members. If your family didn't know you, who did? Nevertheless, Ernest knew God preferred business references. United Way would carry some weight with God, and Ernest had required his employees to give their fair share. Except executives who had special expenses — fashionable clothes, respectable automobiles, meaningful club memberships. He had always donated his unfashionable ties to the Salvation Army; that would be a good reference. He tipped generously at the country club; the employees would speak well of his good sportsmanship, cheerful disposition and socially acceptable habits. God wouldn't listen to Benny. What was he doing there anyway? Benny was a suicide.

Now, the clincher. "I have never done anything bad." That was daring but how much humility did God expect of a man who founded — co-founded — his own business and turned it into a Blue Ribbon Company? Besides, God had His own problems with employees. He gave Adam and Eve everything they wanted and still they complained.

Being stingy with employees wasn't bad; it was profitable and God-approved. People in high places admired him for it. How much did Albert Schweitzer make? Mother Teresa? Jesus didn't complain about being underpaid. Ernest hadn't read the Bible since Sunday School but he remembered that much. And God didn't tell employers to pay medical insurance; He sent Jesus to heal people, and He could do it again if He wanted to. All those union demands — do this, do that; sometimes Ernest believed Eve was president of the local. They wanted anything you told them they couldn't have.

Getting rid of employees before they lost efficiency was good business. Everyone respected him for that. Except

Benny. Benny had co-founded the company, but Benny was sentimental. He wanted to keep loyal employees but the longer they stayed, the more they were paid. As soon as they felt secure they weren't loyal anymore; they started criticizing management.

Benny wanted to spend time with his family instead of looking after their future the way Ernest had done. Ernest could have taken his family to Disneyland, the Grand Canyon, to Yellowstone; he could have taken Margie to San Francisco, New York and Paris, and he would be deciding whether to look for a job or shoot himself while Benny sat in his office and made vice-presidents of his sons. Didn't the Bible say, "God helps him who helps himself"? While Benny was showing his family Paris, Ernest had helped himself.

People sympathized with Ernest; it was a tough thing he had to do, putting his former partner on the street, refusing to hire his sons. They wouldn't have been happy working for the company anyway, expecting special treatment because they used to come to the office on weekends and holidays pretending they were helping their father but getting in the way. Benny said so himself, that he didn't get as much done because they wanted to talk about girlfriends and what they wanted to be and things that Ernest never had time for. He didn't know that Jenny knew a foreigner when the boy showed up at the door expecting to take her to a prom. A Japanese whose people not only bombed Pearl Harbor, they underbid him on a government contract. His government.

And Terry. He didn't know Terry was majoring in drama or he would have made him change. Margie was supposed to take care of things like that and — he didn't want to say anything bad about Margie in his present condition — but she hadn't been as strong protecting his interests as he had been protecting hers.

Ernest hoped God wasn't listening to his thoughts; a man was entitled to some privacy. Nonetheless, Ernest thought he had not presented a strong claim. He would have to promise improvement and beg for mercy. "Although I have never been especially bad, I can be better. I will require that all employees, including executives, contribute to United Way. I will give my old shirts to the Salvation Army in addition to the ties. Therefore, I request a delay in the implementation of Your plans. Sincerely, Ernest Evans."

And God said, "How much more do you want?" No tornadoes, no lightning bolts, no thunder rolls. Just a voice, not exactly western twang but not deep South either. Simple, direct, soft-spoken English. And strangely feminine.

Then another voice, flatter, midwestern, masculine. "He seems to have stabilized. I thought we had lost him when his heart stopped but it's stronger now. If he pulls through the next twenty-four hours, he should be okay."

Carefully Ernest turned his head. He could move. He opened his eyes. He could see white walls but this tunnel was solid and he was flat on his back. There was an IV in his arm and he could clench his fist although it made him tired. He had almost died. His heart stopped while he was in the tunnel begging for more time. And God said he would be okay if he made it through the next twenty-four hours. No, that was the doctor. God said, "How much more do you want?" Why was medicine so masculinely precise and divinity so femininely vague? Benny had asked Ernest for a little time to get his affairs in order, and Ernest had given him twenty-four hours. Surely God was as merciful. Ernest hoped God was listening to that thought.

"P.S.," he said before God turned His attention to other matters; Ernest was a businessman too and he knew how easy it was to forget solicitations. "I request a minimum of twenty-four hours."

That should do it. Unless he had a relapse. Better make it forty-eight hours. A week; that would give him time to get out of the hospital where his chances were better. Unless Margie had a wreck while taking him home. How many wrecks had she had? She was so indefinite, drove with such hesitancy and indecision that people were always running into her. Nothing serious, just enough to give him high blood pressure and the insurance company delusions of grandeur.

He'd ask Terry to drive him home. No good; Terry always had his eye out the window looking for babes. Bill did accounting while driving and, according to Jenny, during the reproductive act; he'd never had an accident but he had been cited for parallel parking. Okay, Jenny, and he would insist that she not bring the children and that she not talk about opportunities. She was a safe driver when she wasn't being an entrepreneur.

Unless a drunk driver ran a red light, crashing into his side of the car, killing him instantly. If he was going to be blind-sided by a drunk driver he wanted to die instantly and not lie broken on the sidewalk until his week was up.

God was on a different time sheet. Forever was just a day in the sight of God, the Bible said. Why not ask for forever? However, forever could be a long time. God didn't say what kind of years they would be. Ernest didn't want to live forever if he didn't know where he was, if some stranger was going to spoon food into his mouth. "I'm just thinking out loud," Ernest said, in case God was listening.

Fifty more years. That should be enough. That would give him time to take Margie to San Francisco and the kids to Disneyland. Maybe take the grandkids to Astroworld. He should be able to count on twenty, twenty-five years of reasonable health. He was doing okay now. His mind was functioning; he was reasoning okay. He could turn his head, couldn't he? He didn't want to live twenty-five years if he couldn't turn his head.

Ernest didn't think it fair that he had to make a decision while he was under the influence of drugs, monitors and medical cupidity, but life had never been fair to Ernest, having to contend as he did with local, federal and divine regulators. God had asked him how much time he wanted and he had better come up with the right number because too many things could go wrong. If he wanted twenty-five years, he'd better ask for twenty-five years. And take good care of himself to lessen chances that some of those years would be spent in pain or living oblivion. He wanted the years to be painless but not too painless. God was tricky. All He promised was a little time.

Twenty-five years. Or was thirty better? He didn't want a lot of years if Margie wasn't there to answer the door and the telephone, make his excuses, buy Christmas and birthday presents for the children and play with the grandchildren. He didn't want to be around if Terry and Bill forced him to give up the company, his office, his interests to make room for themselves and their children. He didn't want them taking his car, selling his home and putting him in a nursing home when he could take care of himself. He didn't want Jenny borrowing money to start her own company and never paying it back. He didn't want them avoiding him when he was dying.

Ernest had never trusted God's goodwill because as far as he could see people who attended church and gave money to charity suffered the same misfortunes as everyone else — not a sound return. Now, he was suspicious of a trap. His mother, father and Benny had been bad-mouthing him to God behind his back, trying to get even. They wanted God to give him time, as much time as he asked for, to live miserably, helplessly, at the mercy of his wife and children.

How, when did he become so vulnerable? He had better set God straight on some things; he had his reasons, good reasons.

"P.P.S. It has come to my attention that I am not in full compliance with divine policy for reasons which I will attempt to clarify to Your entire satisfaction. I did not visit my dying father or ask his forgiveness for fear he would curse me for never repaying the loan and never explaining why I could not work for him. I did not ask forgiveness of my mother because she said she would not speak to me again after I tied her cat to the bumper of the car to take it to the pound. If she hadn't forgotten her umbrella and demanded that I go back in the house and get it, I wouldn't have tied the cat to the bumper. Or have forgotten about it being there. I didn't think Benny would shoot himself; I thought he would start a new business for his sons. I was waiting until I could congratulate him on learning from his error."

That should convince anyone who had ever tried to do business with the kind of people he and God had to work with. Now he needed to be humble.

"Therefore, I request that You convey to them my apology for any wrong I did them and ask them to forgive me for any default. If this transaction meets with Your full approval I will compensate my wife and children for any wrong I might have done them by living a better life than I have lived. I will also teach them the lesson I have learned."

He had learned his lesson. He was going to spend a lot of time with his family, make the most of every moment with them and not count on the future. That was the problem; he could count on the future. At least, he could count on however much time he asked for. He couldn't count on his family learning the lesson he had just learned or listening to him when he had never listened to them. If they did, if his life became better than anything he had known, the closer he got to the last year, the more dread he would feel.

The truth was, he didn't want to die now but neither did he want to decide how much time he had left. Maybe God knew best and adding years to his life was not so good as he had thought.

"Letter to God to supersede the previous letter," he dictated to God who was acting as both scrivener and scorekeeper, who as scrivener was not only omniscient but omnipotent and as scorekeeper was not only explicit but exorable.

"Dear God: In reference to Your inquiry, I request sufficient time to improve my situation and to instruct my family toward standardization regarding Your policy." With a little luck and good health, he could be the kind of father and husband whose family wouldn't neglect him. How long would that take? Fifty years or was he back to forever? He wondered if it was too late. What if they were as unforgiving as his mother and father, as Benny? What if his family didn't listen until they were in a situation similar to his present one?

"Dear God: Please disregard previous communication." He took a deep breath, as deep as he could take in his condition. "I await Your will." That was the right thing, wasn't it? Trusting God. He was finished then with no leftover business, except —

"P.S. If You decide I am to live, I forgive in advance my wife and children, and those of Benny, for anything they may do to me while I am weak or helpless. Faithfully Yours, Ernest Evans."

Living with the Hyenas

Well, Albert, what will I do now with you here in your grave, she thought as she pulled steadily at the weeds. And Stella over there living with hyenas. Phloreene was amazed at how the weeds had grown in three weeks. The wonder of spring rain. And some of them would have been wildflowers too.

The weeds were higher than she had ever seen them in all the years she and Albert had come to that solitary place to clean the graves of his parents. About the only time he left the house was to clean his parents' graves, and now he was in his own. He had spent almost his entire life in the cemetery.

Poor Albert. Tears of gratitude came to Phloreene's eyes. She had married her only chance. She hadn't loved him, not at first anyway, but she was so grateful that he had saved her from being one of those women that men joked about and little boys teased that they had both accepted it as love.

Every day of her married life she had gotten up early to make biscuits and then waited for his nod of approval. And it had never been more than that. Now she wasn't so particular anymore. At first, after Albert died, she had baked the biscuits hoping someone would come by to eat them, and then she just stopped entirely.

She had been so embarrassed the first time she went to the store and bought canned biscuits. She knew she had flushed by the way Coy Tuck had looked at her. She hadn't felt like that since the first time she had bought Cardui, and Coy — he had only been a pimple-faced boy then working in his father's store — had winked at her. She hated him for knowing, first when she was pubescent, then when she ceased being fertile, and now that she was a widow, for knowing she had stopped doing those things that had made her a wife.

"You musta plumb wore out your rolling pin," Coy said with that high-pitched howl he thought was laughter. "I hope it wasn't on Albert."

After Albert's death it had taken her several days to find something to do with herself in the mornings. Finally she started taking her coffee out on the porch and looking over the country the way Albert had. "I don't think there's anyone living on the Obenhaus place anymore," he'd say. He never went to see and she hadn't either.

Poor Albert. He had never cursed her or hit her the way some men did their wives. He had never humiliated her with other women. He had never asked her to be pretty for him, or entertaining, or informed. But he expected her to be busy. He couldn't stand to see her hands idle. If she sat down he always asked her to fetch something for him. He never liked to go any place he'd never been, or do anything different. And the time she made chicken cacciatore, she never did get him to taste it. Albert didn't like anything foreigners ate. He told her never to pull a trick like that on him again. He didn't want no surprises.

Their daughter had been surprise enough. Just the one child and that one a girl. And he thought she had spoiled Stella and taught her to be ashamed of them and their way of life. Stella always wanted something different. Something better. Lord only knew where she was now.

Every year the county gave an award to the mother of the most children, and Phloreene had always hated that time, seeing other women with their children, distended like brood mares, puffed up like spreadin' adders. And all the men elbowing each other and gloating, acting like they had done something. Albert shame-faced as though she had betrayed him. Only a daughter and that one not a natural child. That's what he always said.

"Why couldn't you raise a natural daughter that would get married to some man that could help me and have kids that would give you something to do?" he used to ask.

Stella had always had her nose stuck in a book, and as Albert said, it was Phloreene's fault; she had encouraged Stella to read, even borrowed books for her. Stella was good in school and she had gone off to college. Albert didn't like that. No need in it, and it gave her funny notions. He wouldn't help Stella, but the college let her go free. Albert didn't like that either. Not their place.

Stella didn't come home much when she was in college and when she did, she and her father always fought. He was afraid she would marry a city boy, maybe from a different state. When Stella told him she wasn't going to be a teacher, Albert had been furious. "Zoology? You gonna work in a zoo? You have to go to college to throw hay at elephants and shovel camel manure? I could have taught you right here if you had gotten your nose out of them books."

Stella said she wasn't coming home anymore, but she did. Once. Before she went off to study hyenas in some place in Africa. Albert didn't know much about hyenas, but he knew that decent people didn't have a whole lot of respect for them. He raged that his daughter preferred living with hyenas to getting married, having children and living a natural life.

"Why, they're nothing but scavengers, taking leftovers from lions. And laughing. That's what they're called, 'laughing hyenas'," he snorted.

Stella wrote from time to time, mostly about the hyenas. They were sturdy if ugly beasts, she wrote. Although scavengers, they also preyed on the weak and had been known to bring down old lions. They had massive teeth and jaws that splintered the strongest bones. Phloreene shuddered at the thought of Stella being caught in such jaws.

Albert scoffed at Stella's letters. She wrote that hyenas were not related to dogs and that according to a native myth every hyena was both male and female. "I've never been to college or to Africa either but I know that hyenas are dogs," Albert yelled. "And even the most ignorant man alive knows that nothing is both male and female. It ain't natural. You are either a male or a female and that's all there is to it."

Albert insisted that Stella's letters were not natural. She never wrote about recipes, children or sewing circle. Albert wouldn't have read the letters if Stella had written about recipes; nevertheless, sometimes he said he was sorry they had a daughter. "Maybe if there had been more children you wouldn't have had the time to ruin the one we did have," he said.

Stella didn't know her father had died until he was already in his grave. Albert would have insisted that it wasn't natural, but Stella didn't have a telephone and it took weeks for her to get a letter. She couldn't have come anyway, but she asked her mother to come see her, even offered to pay her way. Phloreene thought about it sometimes and when she did her heart froze. She would have to drive to Wichita Falls, catch a bus to Dallas, an airplane to God knew where. And there were lions and gorillas, and she'd be living with hyenas and sleeping on the ground with snakes. She was lonely, but she was familiar with loneliness, almost comfortable.

Phloreene gathered up the weeds, the dried-up flowers from her last visit and the trash that had blown up around the grave and placed them in the cardboard box she had brought for that purpose. She wondered what they had done with the trash barrel. She stood up, gingerly straightened her back and looked around. She saw a man in blue overalls bent over a grave. "Yoo hoo," she called softly. "I wonder if you could tell me what I'm supposed to do with this."

The man came over, took the box and dumped it behind the little shed. He was polite, but she didn't mean for him to do it. He came back and handed her the box. He was about her age, but tall and straight. "Thank you," she said. "I could have done it myself."

He smiled down at her. It was a nice smile. He had all his teeth and they were clean. "Don't get much chance to help a pretty lady anymore," he said. He hadn't gone to fat or terminal wrinkles the way some men did. "Not since I buried my wife. Maynard Brewster is my name." She recognized the name as a respected one on the other side of the county. A landed farmer, Republican, probably a Baptist. The Brewsters weren't cheerful, good-time folks.

Maynard took off his hat — his hair was clean — and used it to point at a bouquet of gravestones. "Them are Juanita's folks over there, but I put her over here with my family. She'll be on one side of me and my mother on the other."

"How nice," Phloreene said.

"I been working on the graves, her family's and mine, all morning, and I'm plumb tuckered out."

"I got a little something in the basket," she said. She was tired of the house — Lord, it seemed like she had spent her whole life there, so she had brought a picnic to eat under a shade tree. "I'd be proud to share with you," she said. She hadn't talked to anybody in weeks. Besides this was — she shivered a little inside — an adventure.

"I thank you kindly," he said.

He led her to a part of the cemetery she had never visited before. She wasn't one for reading tombstones but one caught her eye. "Henry Holcomb. February 14, 1908, November 7, 1959. Fathered 31 children." Fifty-one years old. Fool man killed himself fathering kids. And how many women did he wear out? she wondered. How many women had he sent to their graves?

And who could have put that on his gravestone? "Fathered 31 children." Certainly not his wives. She couldn't find a monument to a one of them. Nothing about mother of twenty children, or fifteen, or twelve. And certainly his children hadn't put such a thing on his marker. They would have put "reared 31 children" or "provided for 31 children." Why would anyone be proud of something that came as effortlessly to a man as tears to a woman? As naturally too. And who had done the harvesting? she wondered. Who had watered and weeded the crop?

No, no one but a man would have been puffed up about that, she decided. Probably the old scoundrel had asked that a testimony to his seeding be written on his tombstone and his lodge brothers had complied. She could see the pack of them laughing at how lodge brother Henry Holcomb had plumb wore himself out seeding children.

Without having ever known the man Phloreene disliked him, and imagined him sitting out on the porch fanning himself and ordering his wife around — she limping on swollen feet and bumping into things with her extended belly. Poor, disheartened, ill-used thing. Phloreene disliked her too.

Maynard had picked a spot under a post oak tree, put down a gunny sack he had used to kneel on while weeding the graves, placed the basket on it and was waiting impatiently for her. "What were you studying?" he asked. Delicacy forbade her to answer that she had been studying how easy it was for a man to make a memorial to himself. She hurried to open the basket and invited him to eat.

They talked about the spring rain and all the wildflowers, and she didn't mind too much that he scarcely noticed how she was eating carrot sticks because he had helped himself to the sandwich. Men were just that way. She remembered the times when there wasn't much to eat and she had tried to hide from Albert how little she was eating so that he could have all he needed for the hard work on the farm. She had been surprised how easy it was to convince him that she wasn't hungry and that she really preferred chicken necks with sometimes a wing for a special treat and that she didn't really like the cake.

Her mother had brought the cake as a token of appreciation that her daughter had gotten a man. It had been a five-layered chocolate cake. Phloreene had gotten pleasure out of watching the way Albert ate, smacking his lips and sucking his teeth to show his enjoyment. She had suffered guilt for months for having taken a piece of the cake while he was at work, after having vowed that he could have every bite of it.

She was certain that he looked at her strangely that night when she put the cake before him and he cut off a double portion. But he didn't chide her, and she was so grateful and felt so kindly toward him that he had called her "silly" in bed that night.

"I think we met," Maynard was saying about Albert. "Kind of pleased with himself, wasn't he?" They had met. "Like he done what he wanted to do." It was Phloreene Albert hadn't been pleased with. And Stella.

"Every man wants to create a masterpiece before he dies," Maynard said. How nice, Phloreene thought. She didn't think Albert wanted to create a masterpiece. He certainly never said anything about it. "But we never had a son. We kept trying," Maynard said. He sighed. "I guess she did the best she could. Had four daughters. They are all married and got kids. Juanita did right by them that way." Phloreene felt a twinge of fear. "How many grandkids you got?"

"Stella, our only child, is in Africa," Phloreene said and hesitated. "She lives with hyenas."

Maynard stared at her for a moment and she was certain he was going to say it wasn't natural, but his thoughts were elsewhere. "She was a good woman." Maynard was talking about his dead wife. "I'm going to miss her cooking. This here sandwich was real good too. Course I don't eat much bought bread. Hard on the bowels." He patted his bowels.

"I'm sorry. I didn't bake yesterday," she said, feeling flustered. Buy a loaf of bread and everybody in the county knew about it.

"Pretty fair eating," he said, wiping his mouth on the napkin and handing it to her to put away instead of putting it in the basket himself. "I haven't been eating so well lately except when one of my daughters brings something."

"I'll bet you're a good cook," she said and saw the flare of anger in his eyes.

"I'm a man," he said, and when she didn't reply he softened a little. "A man needs someone to see that he eats right and has clean clothes to wear. And a woman needs someone to protect her."

That sounded so nice that Phloreene wanted to snuggle into Maynard's arms and be protected. From what? a little voice nagged. "I was married for forty years and the only thing Albert protected me from was spinsterhood," she said.

"Well, a woman needs someone to take her places."

"I got a car."

"Juanita didn't drive, no need for her to. She didn't go gallivanting around the country like some women do. If she needed to go somewhere I saw to it that she got there on time and got home safe."

Phloreene started to explain but thought better of it. It was her car and she could go anywhere she wanted to. Why, she could go to Wichita Falls if she wanted to. The thought almost took her breath away. She wouldn't know how to drive in Wichita Falls. She wouldn't know where to park. The one time Albert took her to Wichita Falls, he forbade her to cross the street for fear she would get lost.

"I reckon I'm talking about companionship," he said. "Being there when you're sick and when the kids don't write and when you just want to tell somebody about the rain or such."

Phloreene was surprised at the tug she felt. The nesting instinct was still there. She had almost forgotten how strong it had been when Albert had come courting. If he had kissed her one more time, or her mother had delayed bringing them lemonade, why, she might not have been fit for anybody to marry. Of course Albert wasn't very romantic. Not that he didn't like his pleasure, but he didn't want no surprises. But there was a certain gleam about Maynard. Made her feel a little guilty, just enough to enjoy it.

"I don't know how many years I got left and I want to do things," Maynard said. "I aim to learn leathercraft."

She too wanted to do things. And it wasn't too late, not if she didn't let it be too late. "Have you ever thought about going to Wichita Falls and eating in a restaurant?" she asked, feeling breathless at being so bold.

"I don't drive in Wichita Falls," he said. "The people there try to run country folks off the road. And I wouldn't eat in no restaurant when I got a daughter that lives in Burkburnett. I'd just call her and tell her to come get me. She'd feed me and put me up in the kids' room."

She would drive to Wichita Falls and eat in a restaurant by herself. And if she got lost . . . she could feel her heart thumping against her thin chest. She'd go to a service station and ask some man —

"I thought maybe if you was a mind, I might drop by some evening and talk for a spell," Maynard said.

About supper time, Phloreene thought. But she was tired

of eating alone, being alone, with no one to talk to and nothing to do. Cooking for Maynard would be something to do and she could please him with her biscuits; she was certain of that. She thought for a moment of Coy Tuck's face when she bought baking soda. He'd know she was seeing a man.

She would drive to Wichita Falls and eat in a restaurant, and if she got lost she would stop at a service station and ask some man for directions. And if he looked at his friends and they all shook their heads and laughed the way they did when a woman was helpless?

"I don't mind bringing something," Maynard said. "Long as it's not wine. I've never tasted alcohol and I don't never intend to. And I don't favor none of them fancy foreign dishes neither."

She would drive to Wichita Falls and eat at a restaurant and have wine if she wanted it, and if they laughed at her when she asked directions she would drive around until she found her way home. Sleep in the car if she had to. And if a policeman charged her with being vagrant? She would tell him —

"I can't come on a Thursday," Maynard said. "I watch the television Thursday night."

— I got plans. "I thank you kindly, but I got plans," she said. And if the policeman asked her what plans?

"What plans?" Maynard asked, his jaw set like he was going to start laughing.

If she could drive to Wichita Falls, she could catch a bus to Dallas, and fly. . . . Her heart caught in her throat —

"To go places I've never been," she said.

"You've never been nowhere."

— fly to Africa and see Stella, and maybe even — "That's why I'm going now."

"Woman like you can't travel alone," he said. "You don't know the first thing about traveling, and if you got someplace you wouldn't know how to take care of yourself."

— maybe even live with the hyenas. Her stomach knotted. If she could lived with Albert for forty years, maybe for a little while she could live with hyenas. "I can take care of myself," she said.

Maynard threw back his head and laughed.

She had lived with them her whole life.